Descendant of Shadows

DAUGHTER OF DESTINY

Keira F. Jacobs

CHAPTER ONE

Naomi and Hux sat side by side on the wet sand. The sea swelled in front of them, monstrous waves crashing, sending spits of water into the air to dampen their hair and skin. The wood cottages lining the shore behind them were just as damp. The main town of Blaire was two miles inland and its ports were five miles up the shore, leaving these seaside farms to go about their business with no travelers trampling through their lands. It was for this reason that Hux and Naomi landed here, a place where they could hunker down without being hunted until it was time to head back to Le'Gar.

A sword stuck out of the sand next to Naomi. She was still trying to catch her breath after Hux had demolished her in another sword-training session. Her footwork was trash and she had to make up for it with her swings. She was always dripping with sweat before Hux even took a semi-labored breath during their spars. He liked to take their training sessions to the shore. The sand made it more challenging. For Naomi, at least. Though today a drop of sweat fell from Hux's brow during the last spar, and it made Naomi grin.

She draped her aching arms over her knees and stared out

at the water—a force that moved with freedom. She longed for such freedom.

Hux reached into his bag and pulled out an orange. He held it up to her. "Do you mind?"

She held her palm up and smirked.

He placed the fruit in her hand. "Why are you smiling?"

"It's just comical," she said, digging her fingers into the peel. "That you can whip my tail in sword fighting but you can't peel an orange."

"I can peel an orange, but you can do it faster." He held up his right arm. From the elbow down it curled in toward his body, a birth defect resulting in paralysis. "It takes me forever with this, and I'm hungry now."

She worked the peel away and split the fruit in half, placing Hux's share in his good hand. "Does it truly never bother you?"

"That I can't peel an orange?" He popped a slice in his mouth.

She nodded at his right arm that sat across his lap. "That you were born with a disadvantage."

He laughed low, gentle. "Everyone is born with a disadvantage. You can just see mine."

She leaned into him a bit, letting her shoulder touch his. "You should teach me how to view life as you do."

He looked down at her. "Are you feeling beaten down?"

"I suppose I feel down," she admitted, staring ahead into the waves once more. "It's been a month since we left Ferrin and Vira in Mira Isla, and the last we saw of them, Vira was fighting for her life with an arrow sticking out of her chest."

He followed her gaze, nodding. "Ferrin may have healed Vira. We don't know what happened yet, Omi. We have to remain hopeful."

"It took us three days to get here. It shouldn't take Ferrin and Vira a month."

"We don't know what happened after we left Mira Isla. There are a multitude of things that could be keeping them there."

"Like what?" Naomi tried to remain calm, but her voice wavered. "Like the death of Vira? Or the capture of Ferrin? Saul was still in Mira Isla when we left, and he's loyal to King Tal and the city of Le'Gar. Saul is Le'Gar's Lead Rider for goodness sake. If King Tal ordered the capture of Ferrin, Saul will stop at nothing to arrest Ferrin and drag him back to Le'Gar. Truly, Hux, you can't tell me that you aren't worried."

"Of course I'm worried." He closed his eyes, sighing. "But we have to focus on what we can do in the meantime. Like how we've been improving your sword work. Which, by the way, you made me sweat today."

She perked up, smug, shrugging her shoulders. "I did notice that. And I do admit that I am very satisfied by it."

"You're improving," he confirmed. "No doubt. Which is important. Our time here is not for nothing."

"But eventually it will become a blip of time that is useless," she said, her voice catching. "If we are here too long and no one shows up."

Hux let out a long whoosh and leaned forward, as if trying to feel the power of the sea. "What would you suggest then? Are you ready to move?"

She looked sideways at him. "I'm not the warrior."

"But you're the key," he countered. "You might be the only one who can stop the Dark Hand from stealing our world. You can make decisions, too."

Decisions. She had never had the option to make decisions. Not even regarding her own identity. It was a sweet taste, to choose. To have control.

"I can't do anything apart from the quill," she reminded him.

The quill was what started this whole adventure. Unlike a real feather, this quill was made entirely of gold, but it still flowed like a feather would. It was clearly from the realm of the gods—the Outer Void—and if a person from the Massoud bloodline had the quill in his or her possession, the quill was a type of weapon. Naomi just didn't know how to use it yet, though she had discovered, on accident, that the necklace she had worn since she was a child held magical ink for the quill. It was because of this finding that she left the quill with Ferrin while she left Mira Isla, keeping the necklace with her. She figured that separating the two items could protect her, her friends, and the world somehow. She didn't think that having all the powerful items in one place was a wise idea.

"You can manipulate nature with just your thoughts. You don't need the quill to do that," Hux said.

This was true, but she hadn't been able to stir nature since her last night in Mira Isla. All this time in Blaire with Hux, nature seemed to ignore her. Or she just kept failing. One or the other.

She shook her head. "The quill is the most important part of saving our world. I don't know how I'm supposed to use the quill, but if it wasn't so important, your king wouldn't have sought it out, you wouldn't have run away with it when you found it, and my king wouldn't have panicked about the quill being found in the first place." Her throat tightened. "I only hope that leaving the quill with Ferrin didn't put him in more danger than he already is." The thought of him filled her heart with sorrow. Or more so, his absence did.

Hux gave her a knowing glance. "You've been thinking about him a lot, haven't you?"

A red face gave her away. "He's similar to me. Can you blame me for wanting him back? He was going to teach me how to use my powers. I was going to show him that not everyone is out to harm him. We had a deal going. We had—"

"You had something growing between the two of you," Hux interjected. "It's okay, Omi."

She glared. "It was nothing, Hux. We were just similar souls."

"You say 'were' like he's gone."

"He might be," she whispered.

They sat in silence, both watching the water, both mourning their own missing partners.

"I'm sorry." Naomi put a hand on his arm. "I'm complaining when Vira may, too, be gone. I'm being insensitive."

He laid his heavy hand over hers. "We're both worried. And that's okay."

"Did you love Vira?"

The question seemed to take him by surprise. "I do. I always will. But that doesn't mean we are bound to each other. She may go her own way and I may go mine."

"And you're okay with that?"

"Okay?" He chuckled. "No one is ever okay. Even in your happiest times you will find something to not be okay about. Embrace today, Naomi. Find the good. Find the *one* good thing. Otherwise, you'll never be okay. Life is harmful, but it's always fantastic. You get to choose which side to live on."

In that moment, Naomi saw her papa's face behind Hux's passionate expression. He was so much like her papa. Zealous for life. Enthusiastic about the future. Level-headed. She had nearly forgotten what her father looked like, but now, listening to Hux, she got a glimpse again.

Hux must have seen it in her eyes, because he frowned. "Are you alright?"

She threw her arms around his neck and hugged him tight, nearly knocking him backward.

He caught her, his sturdy frame keeping them both upright.

"I'm sorry," she said, squeezing her eyes shut. "I just feel so lost."

He tightened his arm around her. "It's okay. We all get lost sometimes."

———

They left the shore when the sun changed to the golden color of evening. Dinner was already on the table when they entered the cottage that sat at the bottom of the rolling green hills.

An older woman with rough hands and broad shoulders stood in the kitchen doorway. "You're both soaking."

Hux shed his cloak and hung it on the hook by the door. "The surf was choppy today. Lots of mist."

The woman wiped her muscular hands on her apron and strode to the kitchen's hearth. She used a rag to lift a kettle from over the fire and brought it to the table to fill two mugs of water. "There," she said. "What kind of tea would you like then?"

Naomi sat at the table, the smell of the roast on her plate making her mouth water. "It's okay, Emilia. We can get the tea."

"Not in my house," she countered, already shuffling through the cupboard full of tins of loose-leaf tea. "You're guests."

Hux sat next to Naomi. "Guests who have overstayed our welcome."

Emelia placed three tins of tea on the table. "There is no such type of guest. You needed help. I have the space. And I understand that your whereabouts must be kept a secret." She opened one of the tin's lids. "Orange tea?"

Naomi nodded. "That's just fine."

She scooped the leaves into a metal steeping ball and set it in Naomi's water before turning to Hux. "You like the black tea, don't you? The kind that makes you jittery."

He chuckled. "You've learned me well."

She got his tea situated, then sat across from them at her own plate.

Naomi's shoulders sagged. "You didn't have to wait for us to eat."

Emelia rested her palms on the table. "I'm a widowed farmer's wife. I miss eating with someone."

Naomi smiled, cutting into her meat. "Well, thank you again for another meal. We have no words."

"Then don't give me words. I don't need them. I can sense good in you two. Something this world needs." Her fork clinked against her plate as she sighed, then clasped her fingers together. "Which is why I'm saddened to tell you this."

Naomi looked up, half a mouthful of roast still needing to be chewed.

Hux leaned forward. "Tell us what?"

"I heard that Riders are headed this way."

The roast in Naomi's mouth suddenly wanted to come out, but she forced it down. "Riders from where?"

"The folks who saw them said the man leading the crew had a Le'Garian chestplate."

Saul.

"Where were they seen?" Naomi pressed. "Are they already in Blaire?"

"Most likely," Emelia confirmed. "May be holed up in town."

Hux dropped his head into his hands.

"We need to go," Naomi whispered, feeling a lump in her throat.

"Now wait." Emelia held a hand up. "The only way out of here is back through town. Unless you want to take a shipping boat to who knows where. If you stay put, I can cover for you as best I can."

"It's a kind gesture," Hux admitted, "but we can't just wait to be found. We need to move while we still can."

Emelia twisted her linen napkin between her fingers. "You may be right. But wait two more nights. It'll be a new moon. Less light. You can leave unnoticed."

Hux nodded, a sorry smile plaguing his lips. "You've been so kind. We hate to go."

"I hate it, too." Emelia swallowed. "You two are gonna do something special, aren't you?"

Naomi felt tears in the corner of her eyes. "We sure hope so."

CHAPTER TWO

Saul led his horse into the dawn-lit forest surrounding the city of Mira Isla. His shoulders and biceps ached, but not as much as his damaged pride. Only three of his Riders remained alive after invading Mira Isla in search of Naomi Massoud, Ferrin, and Hux, the treasonist from Raina. The occupants of Mira Isla had fought back with much more force than he'd anticipated. As Lead Rider of Le'Gar, Saul had made the decision to retreat, and ordered his remaining Riders to flee to the forest moments before he galloped away from the city. He had yet to find his Riders, but he believed in their ability to stay hidden, and he knew they would be waiting for his next command. Of course, his next command would be to slip out of Mira Isla unnoticed. Those he came here seeking had not been found. The invasion only led to loss of life. Even the two others he had been riding with—Maya, the Lead Rider of Raina, and Estell, the golden witch—were nowhere to be found. He presumed them dead as well.

Saul pulled his horse sideways and kicked the stallion into a trot. Autumn fell around him in dark gold leaves fluttering to the ground. They glinted in the rising sun and he watched one sway like a cradle all the way to the damp ground.

Fingers poked through the dirt.

His chest lurched

A buried body.

He dismounted and bent down to examine the fingers. They were frail spindles with dirt lodged beneath the nails, and they still held a decent amount of color. Not pale like a dead body should be.

Cautiously, Saul trailed his finger along the slender digits. He yanked his arm back when they twitched and clutched at him.

Recollecting himself, he groped for the hand and began to tug. It was too easy. The dirt gave way effortlessly. Before he knew it, an entire arm was visible and then the top of a head. When he saw the white hair, his yanks became more desperate. He knew this body. He knew this golden witch.

Her body morphed out of the ground, dirt spilling like an avalanche. She sputtered, coughing up the soggy soil. Saul kept pulling until her feet were free, then dropped to his knees to hold her steady.

She clung to his arms, still gagging.

"E," he spoke with much more care than he meant to show. "What happened to you?"

When she looked at him, both eyes were dark like her pupil. The sight of them struck Saul's core.

"The Massoud," she spat. "She tried to drown me in the soil, just like she will do to all of Thãen."

Though her stare was unnatural, Saul couldn't help but see a fleck of hurt. "Naomi Massoud is truly evil," he whispered.

Estell leaned into him. "She took my lover as her own and tried to destroy me."

Saul held her against him, but frowned. Her lover? Surely

she couldn't be talking about Ferrin. Saul had heard the story about Ferrin's treason in Le'Gar, and that story involved a love interest of his as well. A golden witch named Estell. But this golden witch had told him that her name was E. That was all she gave him, and he never questioned her until now. But now he finally made the connection. E. Estell. She was the golden witch that Ferrin had fallen in love with.

Saul sat back, holding Estell in front of him by her arms, forcing eye contact. "You're Estell?"

"I am."

"But Ferrin loved you over one hundred years ago. Golden witches aren't immortal." He searched her pristine face. "You shouldn't be alive."

"Yet I am. Because I'm fighting for a better Thãen. One where Calamity rules."

Saul released her, rising to his feet. "No."

She scrambled up after him. "Listen, Rider." She softened her voice. "Saul."

He stared down at her. Something in her glittering eyes made him keep his mouth shut.

She stepped forward, placing a hand on his chest. "If we surrender to Calamity now, we won't be subjected to slavery when Thãen inevitably shifts from the palm of Protection to that of The Dark Hand. We will be an equal. A figure of authority."

His heart thudded hard beneath her palm. His vision blurred. His veins chilled. "If Calamity takes us, we won't own ourselves."

"Unless we willfully submit," she persuaded. "If we turn to Calamity, we will be spared the slavery."

"And what of our life now?"

A gentle grin took over her lips. "What of it?"

He watched her move closer, feeling her presence in a way

he used to long for. The feeling of someone tender instead of brash. Gentle instead of authoritative.

"What do you have to lose?"

"Nothing," he answered, feeling the pain of that reality. He truly had nothing. Being Lead Rider was his everything. That was all.

"Then cross over to my side." She leaned in. "From rags to riches."

He breathed in her tempting warmth. "I don't come from rags."

"But you will wear nothing *but* rags when Calamity finally rules. Decide now, and power will be yours." She moved in closer, her nose almost touching his.

He withdrew, though it took all his effort. "What will you gain if I do?"

She sighed but allowed him another smile. "You. Don't you see? I'm lonely on this side. I need a partner."

Something in his chest pulled. Something tried to draw him away from her. He knew the feeling was knowledge. Knowledge of right and wrong. But she was here. Power was here. At the end of the day, he believed in every man for himself. If he gave in to her, he would have everything he ever wanted. Power and a companion. "Show me your side," he accepted. "I want a taste of something different. Something better."

She smiled against his nose. "Done."

CHAPTER THREE

Naomi turned over to her side. The window in the room she was sleeping in faced the sea. She could hear waves swell and crash. Even the thrum of their movements she could feel. It was as if the water called to her. But what had actually woken her was a slight tremble. A vibration, as if the world was rocking.

She sat up. It was still dark outside, but she couldn't fall back asleep. Movement stirred within her. Thãen had trembled, like the rumbling of a stomach. Naomi felt as if the world was saying, *"Get up and fight. This war is about to change."*

The burgundy quilt draped over her legs suddenly seemed heavy. She kicked it off and swung her legs to the floor. Hux was asleep on the other side of the wall in the second spare room. Emelia had multiple rooms in preparation for multiple children. Children which never came, she had revealed one night.

Naomi shoved her feet into her boots. New boots. Also given to her by Emelia. When she had her cloak adjusted at her neck, she grabbed her sword from the corner of her room. She had stolen the sword off one of the Riders of Raina whom Hux had slayed in Mira Isla.

She crept into the narrow hallway and moved slowly so as not to creak the wooden floorboards. In only a few feet, she reached Hux's door and shoved it open, slipping inside. He snored, his shoulders rising and falling under his blanket like a sleeping bear. It may have been intimidating to wake him if she hadn't grown so close to him in the last month. But she crossed his room and grabbed his shoulder, shaking it.

"Hux," she whispered.

His eyes flung open and he sprang to a sitting position.

Naomi jumped back. "It's me. Hux, it's me."

His shoulders dropped. "For graves' sake, I thought I was going to have to hurt someone. What are you doing?" Then he was focused. "What's wrong?"

"Nothing's wrong." She threw his covers off of him. "Come on. Get up."

He frowned but stood. "Are you okay?"

She grabbed his own sword from beside his bed and thrust it at him. "Put something decent on," she ordered, as he took the sword. "You can't spar in your drawers."

He awkwardly pulled on his linen pants while balancing his sword in the crook of his arm. "Naomi, who am I sparring? Is it even dawn?"

She stood in his doorway, keeping her voice low. "You're sparring me. And no, it's not dawn. But why do we have to wait for Thãen to wake up to train? It'll be more challenging in the dark anyway."

He stumbled after her into the hallway. She felt a grin come on as she pushed open the back door. Something inside of her twitched with anticipation. Jolts of energy shot through her arms. She couldn't get to the beach fast enough, and practically ran down the grassy embankment to the sand. All the way she felt nature prodding her.

Get up and fight. This war is about to change.

Two days. She and Hux had decided last night that they would leave Blaire in two days, when there was a new moon, and head back to Le'Gar. While fleeing Mira Isla, nature had spoken to her, and it told her to go back home to Le'Gar. She had every right to ignore nature and stay away from the city that seemed to want her dead, but in her heart she knew that nature was on her side, and if nature knew that Le'Gar had answers about defeating Calamity, Naomi had to believe nature's voice.

But two days wasn't long, and she wanted to be as skilled in sword fighting as she could be before then.

"Naomi, hang on." Hux jogged to keep up. He stopped when she did, on the shore, only a few feet from the tide. "Face me."

She did, feet apart and sword raised.

"Take one deep breath. The key to being a successful warrior is a calmed mind and a tamed spirit."

She nodded, breathing in through her nose and letting it out again slowly. She did this a few times before Hux raised his own sword. She smiled, excited.

He almost smiled back, but his brows remained furrowed, as if he didn't know what to expect from her.

But she didn't know what to expect from herself either. She had never felt this type of anticipation before. This call to action. "Are we a go?" she asked.

"We're a go."

She swung her sword. He blocked it fast, swishing at her from the other side with fluidity.

"Calm," he said, blocking another swing. "Keep calm."

Breathing in, she felt her muscles relax into place. A place of fluid motion and speed. As if wound up by a key and let go, her wrists rolled and twirled like gears. Her feet moved as if in a dance.

"Good! Good!" Hux shouted, stepping back because she had forced him to.

She kept going, jabbing and swishing. Even blocking. She blocked every one of his shots.

Sweat appeared at his hairline. An expansive grin came with it. "Good, Naomi!"

I'm doing it, she thought. *I'm winning.*

She swung another and he lunged backward. She imagined his foot getting trapped in the sand, and suddenly his leg sunk, holding him hostage. His eyes sprang wide, but he kept blocking her swings.

At the sight of the sand swallowing his foot, she hesitated.

"No," Hux boomed. "Keep going."

She was manipulating nature. It was listening to her again.

Circling around him, she aimed the sword at his back. He deflected it with a twist and a grin.

The tide surround him, she thought. And suddenly her feet were wet. The surf moved in at a rapid pace, rushing around their shins, shifting the sand beneath their feet.

Hux staggered on the moving sand and ripped his foot free. He faced her again.

She stopped, letting the sword drop at her side.

"What are you stopping for?" Hux panted, sword still raised to fight. "You're on the verge of winning."

They both stood in the waves now, knee deep. She had moved the sea from low to high tide with nothing but thoughts. It was meant as an attempt to give Hux the disadvantage, but she had gotten too eager and surrounded herself with water as well. If this were a real situation, she would have doomed herself, too.

"I didn't control it well," she said, tottering as a wave broke against her thigh. "I didn't know how. I don't know how."

She shut her eyes, feeling the sticky sea salt spray on her palms. *You can recede.*

The sea obeyed. It drew back from the shore like a snake recoiling, returning to low tide and leaving Hux and Naomi on fairly solid land again. The first pale light of morning touched the sky, illuminating their shadowed bodies.

"It's the first time you've manipulated nature since Mira Isla," Hux pointed out. "Don't you see that as a good thing?"

She stuck her sword in the sand. "I need to learn to control it if I'm going to use it successfully."

"That's where practice comes in," he offered.

"I need a mentor. You're a fabulous mentor for sparring, but you don't have experience with this kind of power."

A gentle smile touched his lips. "You're thinking about Ferrin again."

She faced the sea, arms crossed. "I can't help it."

Hux picked up her sword and shoved it back into her hands. "Come on."

"What? You want to have another go?"

"I do." He took her shoulders and positioned her to face him again. "We leave in two days, and you need to be ready."

Her stomach dropped. "You're positive you want to go without Ferrin and Vira?"

"We have to. Nature told you to go back there."

"I know, but I feel a bit of hesitation. Le'Gar is the one place that wants me dead."

He huffed. "It's the one place that holds answers. And to be honest Naomi, I think half of Thãen wants you dead. At least, those who know what a Massoud can do."

She tightened her hold on the hilt. "And you think two more days of training will prepare me enough?"

"It's better than nothing." He took a step toward her. "Now raise up your weapon. Fight me, Naomi Massoud."

CHAPTER FOUR

The Draycott Inn was a quiet place. Most people in Mira Isla were permanent residents, having no need for temporary housing. The rooms upstairs were small and nearly always empty, but the tavern on the main floor filled up in the evenings. It was what kept the business running. But for the last month, the Inn had seen more use than usual when it came to housing guests.

Ferrin strode into the tavern, sleep still lingering behind his eyes. The carvings in the wooden beams on the ceiling of the tavern were familiar to him now. Welcoming, even. The long wooden table in the middle of the room was already stocked with fresh scones and coffee. Baylor, the cook, knew by now that Ferrin would have breakfast here. He had for the last month.

The window facing the street was open, letting in fresh morning air. Fall was in full swing and on the verge of dropping to winter, which meant the lands outside of Mira Isla were deep into spring by now.

Ferrin sat at the table, took the ceramic pitcher of steaming coffee and poured himself a mug. He paused with his hand on the mug handle and stared at his knuckles. His gaping wounds were healing, nearly closed up. The cracks in his skin along his forearms were paling, becoming scar tissue. He felt stronger. Whole.

The sound of quick feet drew his attention to the bottom of the stairs that led up to the rooms of the Inn. Vira's eight-year-old daughter Millicent drifted into the room. Her satchel hung at her side and her hair flowed wildly. She hadn't had her hair braided since Vira...

"Hey." Ferrin smirked. "You're late."

She trotted over to him and swiped his coffee mug. "I was up all night trying to do that stupid math equation my teacher says I must know." She took a big gulp of the coffee.

He watched her, unimpressed. "You're going to be jittery. Give me that."

She placed the mug back on the table and grinned. "Want to walk with me to school?"

He gave a sorry smile. "I can't today. I have business this morning."

"That's okay, I understand." She stood on her tiptoes and kissed him on the cheek. "Will you be here when I get back?"

He swallowed, moved by her gesture. "Yes."

Before leaving she grabbed a scone. As she headed out the tavern's front door, Ferrin couldn't help but see how much her hair was in shambles. Matted and tangled. Long and frayed.

He stood. "Hold on."

She stopped in the doorway and turned back toward him. "You said I'm gonna be late."

"I know, but I need to do one last thing." He walked to her and raked his fingers through her hair. As he did so, her hair sprang back to life, gaining shine and losing its knots. It cost him little power to make sure Vira's daughter was taken care of as best he could. He had promised Vira that.

Millicent's face lit up when she realized what he had done. "Thank you!"

He gently shoved her out the door. "Tell your teacher you were late because of me."

She flashed a wide grin at him before bounding into the street, headed toward school.

When Ferrin turned back around, he saw his business sitting at the breakfast table: Maya, Lead Rider of Raina.

"You're good with her," Maya said, spinning a coffee mug between her hands.

Ferrin sat next to her and shrugged. "No child should go through what she has."

Maya stared at him, her dark lips twitching, like she was trying to suppress emotion. "I agree." She dropped her head, sighing. "I've tarried and toiled over what you've asked me to do."

"Have you reached a decision?" he asked, pulse quickening.

"My Riders are itching to leave Mira Isla. They think finding Hux is still the most pressing matter."

"But you don't," he said, hopeful.

"I don't know what I think." She clutched the edge of the table. "You're asking me to commit treason."

"It's not treason. It's a change in mission. A retreat, if you will."

"But we both know Hux is alive and well."

He brought his mug to his lips. "Do we?"

She glared. "This isn't fun and games to me, Ferrin. You are asking me to betray my king's orders."

He smacked a palm on the table. "I'm asking you to go home, tell your king that Hux was never found and the quill is lost."

"Which is a *lie*."

"It's a white lie," he admitted. "But you wouldn't be here if you didn't feel a stirring in your spirit. A sense that what Hux did was necessary."

"His eyes," she whispered, hanging her head. "When I aimed my sword at him, I could read his desperation. He didn't steal the quill because he wanted power. He truly believed the quill in the hands of King Leeland would be dangerous. Does Hux know how the quill should be used?"

Ferrin leaned forward, nodding with vigor. "Yes, Maya. The quill will be of no use in Leeland's hands. It will only work with Naomi because she is part of a sacred bloodline. She's the last of her kind." His heart thrummed, and he took an extra moment to control his facial expression. Maya had to keep believing that Naomi had the quill. If she found out he had it tucked under his clothes against his chest, this conversation could turn for the worse. He had gained her alliance, but not the entirety of her trust. She was still conflicted.

Maya hung her head, shoulders slouching. "I'm not willing to give up my lead position as Hux did."

"I'm not asking you to. Go home. Buy us some time."

She lifted her eyes to him once more. "Tell me what is so special about Naomi Massoud."

"Naomi Smyth," he corrected. "You must call her Smyth."

"Naomi Smyth. Though I don't know why I should keep her identity from my king. He could use her in his plan to rid Thãen of Calamity, could he not?"

Ferrin pressed his fingertips against his mug. "He could also kill her, could he not?"

"Why would he?"

"Because she would be the true savior of Thãen. Not him."

Maya nodded, staring off. "My Riders are eager to go home. I assume King Leeland thinks we're dead. It would make sense for us to leave Mira Isla and return to our own land and calm any uproar that may be happening in our absence."

"So go," he begged. "Buy us time. I will find Naomi and Hux and we will figure out the best way to bring Calamity down, but we have to tread carefully. Starting a war with the Outer Realm could mean destruction to our world. There must be a strategy."

"But what is so significant about Naomi?" Maya pressed. "Do you even know what she's capable of?"

The slightest smile touched Ferrin's lips. "She is a star about to burst. If you spent any time with her, you'd know what I mean. She has power in her veins and purpose in her spirit. She was destined to bring Calamity down."

Maya frowned. "But you have power. You are Ferrin the Magnificent. You can create power from nothing, unlike the golden witches who manipulate power that already exists in some shape or form. Why can't you make a move against Calamity?"

He tapped his chest. "I'm. Not. Her. I don't have Massoud blood."

She nodded, then looked down. "I despise that I trust you."

His heart welled against his rib cage with hope. "So you'll do as I ask?"

"I'll do what I think is right," she amended. "And right now, I think King Leeland may be in over his head and doesn't have Thãen's best interest in mind. Not entirely, anyway."

"I'm only asking you to deter him from his hunt for Hux. That's all. I'm not looking to undercut your king in any way. This is not political, you understand that, don't you? It's life or death."

"I know," she said, hushed. "Which is the only reason I'm agreeing to do what you're suggesting."

His nerves left his body with a shaky breath. "Praise Protection for you, Maya."

She shook her head. "No. I'll not take praise. I brought pain to Mira Isla when my Riders and I invaded, yet your people took in our injured."

He thought of Naomi and felt a wave of worry. He had been fighting away worry since she left Mira Isla with Hux. "No one wants to lose people they care for," he managed to say. "And people with good hearts won't allow suffering to Riders who were merely acting on commands." He paused to clear his throat. "Your Riders didn't choose to invade because they have seeds of evil in their hearts, they invaded because they were told to. A duty."

"We were misled," she said, pinching the bridge of her nose. "By that treacherous golden witch. I hope the ground finished her off."

Ferrin had seen Naomi command the ground to swallow Estell. In mere seconds the woman who had permanently scarred his life was gone. But her face on the way down was something he wished he could forget: honest terror. Because no one is truly capable of being fearless. Not even her.

"I've seen no evidence of Estell," he said. "But Saul and his remaining Riders successfully fled. Either they knew of the secret portal, or they had a golden witch to help them escape through the waterfall."

Maya's expression was stone, nodding in thought. "Estell will kill Naomi."

"But I'll find Naomi first. There is no way I'll let Estell hurt her."

"Good." Maya rose. "Because that woman has true evil in her heart."

His breathing labored. "I know."

Maya stepped away from the table then stopped. She placed her hand on Ferrin's shoulder, his posture slouched in his chair. "We may be from different territories, and we are even a different race, but we both desire the right ending," she said gently. "That's what this is all about."

He nodded, unable to bring his eyes up. "I only hope we can get to the end."

She let her hand fall away and strode to the door. "We will. Just find Naomi Smyth."

Ferrin watched her leave, holding onto her last words. He would find Naomi. He would. Ever since she left, a gaping hole had settled in his chest. He didn't want to admit it, but she had embedded herself in him. She was light and strength, and he was drawn to that. She was humble and unsure, and he wanted to lift her up, put her on a pedestal. And after what Brahm, the magical jewelry maker who resided in Mira Isla as a ghost, told him—that Naomi was a god—he knew that he needed to find her quickly. Because Brahm was right. A god who can't control their powers could be a danger to not only the world, but to themselves.

"What day is it?" a familiar voice said from the bottom of the stairway.

Ferrin shot to his feet, startled. He nearly fell to his knees when she moved away from the stairs and into the main tavern area. This woman had been fighting for her life since an arrow had plunged through her chest. Every day for the past month Ferrin had awakened and crept into her room, hoping with all his sorry might that her eyes would be open. But they never were. She kept breathing, her wound kept healing, but her eyes remained shut and her body stayed rigid. He had poured all of his healing powers into her until his hands split open and his arms ripped with cuts. He almost killed himself trying to save her. And he was starting to believe it was all for nothing, because the golden witch never woke up.

Until now.

"Vira," he whispered, stumbling forward. "Sit down. Sit down. You need to rest."

She stepped into the tavern and held a hand up to him. "Relax, Ferrin, I'm feeling well. Where are the others?"

"They left. They left the night you were hit."

Her dazed expression settled into worry as she focused on Ferrin's face. "What is it?" She took in a short breath. "What's wrong?"

He reached for her hand and when their fingertips grazed, he began to softly cry. "Good graves, Vira, I couldn't look at your daughter anymore, knowing her mother may never wake again."

She placed both of her hands on his shoulders. "You are a saint, ranger."

He laughed through a sniff. "Don't call me that, witch."

"Ferrin the Magnificent," she said softer. "You are a force. I owe you my life." She breathed slowly, bowing her head to his. "You kept watch of my daughter?"

He nodded against her forehead. "I wasn't going to let anything touch her. You don't understand what watching you fight for your life did to me. I respect you now more than ever. I'm sorry for ever being hostile toward you. You didn't deserve any of that, Vira. I'm sorry."

"I forgive you," she reassured, clenching his shoulders even harder. "I hold no bitterness toward you."

"Thank you," he managed to get out. "Thank you."

"Now go pack a bag. We have our other halves to find. And I want to see my daughter."

CHAPTER FIVE

It was the perfect day for a funeral. At least that's what King Tal Demar thought. It was pouring rain and the clouds were thick and suffocating. Every Le'Garian crowded the streets for Tal's father's funeral. It was tradition to send deceased royalty to the sea as their final resting place, a symbol that they were above normal folk and didn't rot in the ground like everyone else, but took a final voyage. The burden of getting the body and coffin to the water was shared by everyone in Le'Gar. The city was built into the mountain, its streets naturally flowing downward as they weaved back and forth. Eventually the streets turned to dirt paths and ended at the docks where the tall ships were housed. The path to the sea was long, which was why the Le'Garians formed a train and passed the coffin over their heads while singing old grave hymns.

King Tal stood on the docks, his cloak soaked from the rain. His wife stood behind him with their three daughters, every single one of them just as drenched. He didn't turn around to look at them as his father's coffin made its way down the last stretch of path in the hands of his people. He knew what kind of eyes he would see from his wife: eyes full of fear.

When Tal had shown his wife, Lita, his father's black hands, she had dropped to the floor and sobbed.

"You're cursed by the Dark Hand, destined to die the same way!" she had cried. *"Our children, Tal! We have placed this on our children!"*

Her screams lived in his head now. All day, every day, every night. Because she was right. His father had died the moment he decided to act against Calamity. There was no escaping The Dark Hand. Not now. Not after their family had served Calamity for decades.

Tal stepped forward and placed his palms on the bottom of his father's coffin, as his Riders—his new Riders—took the sides of the wooden box. Saul and the other Riders never returned after being sent to find Ferrin. Saul was his Lead Rider, and they had grown close in the last couple of years. The absence of Saul weighed heavy on Tal's heart. To have him absent during a death such as this made him aware of the empty place at his side.

Together, Tal and his men carried the coffin across the dock and to the tall ship that waited with a crew ready to set sail. A thick knot clogged his throat as he trudged up the plank into the ship. It didn't feel right. To carry his father on his back, knowing this death had happened not because of sickness, but because of disobedience to The Dark Hand. And to know that he still served the very force that had taken his father.

They lowered the coffin to the ship's deck, and when Tal straightened, he dared to glance back down to the dock at his family. Tears streaked his wife's cheeks and she had both arms wrapped protectively around all three girls. She gave a single nod to him as the crew lifted the sails and broke away from the dock. Tal didn't let his gaze trail from her as the final goodbye hymn drifted from the Le'Garians flooding the mountain.

> *"Farewell, mighty soul.*
> *The sea take you now.*
> *Surrender to death's pull.*
> *No longer crowned.*
> *We will remember your strength,*
> *your power, your lead.*
> *Yet now we say goodbye*
> *and follow your seed."*

Tal was filled with anxiety and the overwhelming sense of responsibility. He had been acting king for the past seven years while his father slowly slipped away with sickness. Le'Gar already followed him, yet now the weight of his duty hit him with full force. These were his people, and they trusted him. They trusted him to keep them safe. The guilt of knowing his own true colors synched his core, and he slid his hand beneath his cloak to the letter tucked in an inner chest pocket. He didn't dare pull it out with everyone around, but he had memorized the words his father managed to write before Calamity took him: *Turn the key but warn Le'Gar. Ring the bell. Let—*

That was it. That was all his father had left for him. A defiant act against Calamity that made no sense. At least not yet.

Tal lifted his chin to the clouds. Rain spat against his face as the ship picked up speed. He wouldn't dare open his mouth in defiance against Calamity or let his fingers show even the slightest deviation from his Master's work. But as far as he knew, The Dark Hand couldn't read his thoughts. So he let his curiosities wander. He would think. He would ponder. He would decipher his father's unfinished letter in secret. And when he did, he would make a decision. To doom his family to immediate death, or doom them to service to Calamity.

———

Eli, the oldest Magnificent alive, and Deirdre Lloyd, Le'Gar's librarian, crouched behind a steeple that peaked above the fog smothering Le'Gar. They had watched the trail of Le'Garians pass Tal's father down to the sea, and remained watching as the ship headed out into the evening waters to deliver the body to the deep. It wouldn't be back until late in the night.

"King Tal is distant. Don't you think, Eli?" Deirdre said with both confusion and hope. "I can see it in his demeanor."

Eli dragged his fingers along the steeple's molding. "I feel it."

She cast a sideways glance at him. "Have you received any visions? Any inkling as to what could have happened to him?"

"No. But let me point out the one thing I think is strange in all of this." He paused, making sure he had her full attention. "I've been alive for two-hundred-thirty-two years, and for all that time, I've lived in Le'Gar. I've witnessed the death of Demar royalty, but not once has the body been sent to the sea without a viewing first."

Deirdre frowned, revealing the hard edges of her jawbone, like that of the gargoyles. "You believe the death of Tal's father is an important piece of the puzzle?"

He nodded. "I believe his body could have shown us something. And perhaps that's what has King Tal in disarray. Perhaps Tal saw something."

"Tal is obviously keeping it hidden if that's the case, so whatever happened to his father, we may never know," she said, forlorn.

"But for how long? He's falling apart. I feel that in my bones.

Something inside of him is about to break. The only problem is, will it be a clean break?" He touched Deirdre's arm, squeezing slightly. "Walk me through the beginning again. Every detail. What are we missing? How are the gargoyles here in our city going to help us defeat Calamity? I feel that we are running out of time."

"The time is coming soon," Deirdre agreed. "I share a special connection with the gargoyles, and they feel a shift in the war with the gods, too. Protection placed the gargoyles in Le'Gar to watch over anyone who may be part of the Massoud bloodline. Their job, right now, is to make sure Naomi Massoud will be safe here in Le'Gar."

"If Protection placed the gargoyles in Le'Gar, then Protection must want Naomi here. Le'Gar must be the place where Naomi can defeat Calamity." Eli stared out at the sea. "We need to get Naomi back to the city."

CHAPTER SIX

Naomi had seen Tal's throat sliced open twice in a recurring dream, and she prayed to never see it again. Her prayers had worked, because she hadn't had the dream since she was in Mira Isla. But a spring storm was brewing across the seaside farm when she lay down for the night, and she felt a stirring in her soul. So when the dream came again that night, she wasn't surprised, only horrified.

In the dream, the cathedral doors blew open as they always did, and Tal's body crashed in behind The Dark Hand. As Tal lay dead on the floor, Calamity rushed in and filled the ceiling. It hovered over her like a black sea. Her heart raced and her limbs trembled, feeling the dark presence as if she were a prisoner waiting to be executed. But something else always happened in this dream. And when she looked through the open cathedral doors out into center square, she saw that something.

Ferrin.

He spotted her, too, only this time he didn't seem shocked to see her. He seemed utterly relieved and desperate. "Naomi!" he screamed.

The air stilled around her. She held her breath and nodded.

"Where are you?" he shouted. "Tell me."

"Blaire," she said, keeping her voice down. "But now it knows." She pointed a finger up at Calamity. "So hurry."

"Leave," he instructed. "We will meet you."

Her whole body jolted. "We?"

Ferrin's cloak flicked in the wind and his legs seemed to evaporate. "I'm waking, Naomi. Find me." His eyes drifted away from her to stare at a space between the cathedral's statues along the wall. He lifted an arm and pointed. "Look out, Omi. Someone is there." Then he woke, leaving the dream.

Naomi whipped her head to the side and caught a glimpse of a blurred face. But she felt herself fading, and suddenly she opened her eyes. The darkness of the room in Emelia's home smothered her and she sat up, waving her hands above her head, imagining Calamity hovering. But she was alone. No king with a sliced throat, no Dark Hand, no Ferrin.

His last words echoed in her mind: *Look out, Omi. Someone is there.*

Her gut wrenched with warmth and longing. He had called her Omi. The name he once refused to use. The name he had never used until now.

"Graves, Ferrin," she whispered, clutching the pendant hanging around her neck. "I miss you." Rubbing her eyes, she remembered something else he had said. *We will meet you.*

We. Vira was alive.

That sent Naomi springing from her bed. Her feet barely hit the floor before she launched into a sprint. For the second time, she thundered into Hux's room and shook him awake. When he opened his eyes and saw her, his expression filled with irritation.

"Oh, come on, Naomi, please don't make me spar in the dead middle of the night," he groaned.

A smile flicked on her lips. "I don't want to spar. I want to leave. Vira's alive."

He sat up and grabbed her. "What?"

"Vira's alive," she erupted, laughing almost hysterically. "Get up! We're moving now. They're going to meet us—"

A bang and a shudder exploded from the kitchen. The sound of the front door slamming open. Hux sprang to his feet and shoved Naomi behind him. Together they stood frozen, listening.

The light sound of footsteps crept through the quiet of the house. It sounded like more than one person was in the kitchen and heading for the hallway. The hallway stretched for the entire length of the house in an L-shape. They could get to the back door if they went now, but Emilia was asleep two rooms down.

"We can't leave her if someone is breaking in," Naomi whispered, barely making a sound.

Hux took a leery step toward the bedroom door. The footsteps just outside were nearing, but a strange, soft, shushing sound accompanied the sound of feet. It sounded as if something was spilling across the floor. Hux nearly sent Naomi flying when he jolted backward. He lifted his foot and shook away a spider that had crawled over his bare toes. When he looked down, more were making their way into the room.

"What in the name of darkness," Naomi hissed. She grabbed Hux's shoes from his bedside and shoved them in his arms. "Get these on and wake Emilia. Be quick."

Hux shoved his shoes on and grabbed his chest plate with Raina's tusked elephant emblem engraved upon it, flicking away more spiders as they skittered toward him. "It's Calamity, Omi. It's here."

Naomi placed her own bare foot near the spiders. *Move,* she thought. They darted out of her way and let her step in a clear space. She smiled, feeling a swell of deviousness. "Get Emilia," she said again to Hux. "I'll buy us time."

"No." He tugged on her shoulder. "We aren't separating."

She met his eyes and stared deep into his worried look. "It's not Calamity." She lowered her voice to a whisper as the footsteps stopped. "It's Estell."

Hux shook his head.

"Yes," Naomi argued. "Emelia said there were Riders in town. No doubt Estell has persuaded Saul and Maya to follow her. Now go, Hux. I'll meet you outside."

"You better have a plan."

"I've got a plan," she reassured. "Get Emelia out."

Hux poked his head into the hall, paused, then sprinted. His massive body thunked down the hallway, drawing the attention of the two intruders in the kitchen. But as he disappeared into Emilia's room, Naomi stepped out into the hallway. Her bare feet found clear spots between the spiders and she latched onto the arachnids with her mind. *Turn around,* she commanded. *Rush the intruders.*

The eight-legged creatures twisted and stumbled over each other as they changed direction. Faster now, they darted back toward the kitchen. They ran in a swarm and the startled grunts and shrieks from the intruders let Naomi know her plan was working.

She watched Hux guide a drowsy Emelia into the hall then morph into the darkness as they rounded the corner to the back door.

"The girl's here!" Estell's voice rasped through shrieks.

Naomi bolted down the hall and past the kitchen.

"There!" Saul shouted.

But Naomi was already at the back door. She stumbled out onto the damp grass and began to sprint up the hillside. Hux's silhouette stood out in the darkness at the top of the hill, Emilia hunched at his side.

"They know I'm here," Naomi panted as she reached them.

"Go now," Emilia ordered.

Naomi shook her head. "What about you?"

Emelia smiled but gave no answer.

Hux twitched, uneasy. "We do need to go. In a few seconds we're going to be found."

Turning around, Naomi faced Emelia's house again. The sand and sea sat right outside the front door.

"Emelia," she said, cringing. "If I give you enough time, will you be able to get somewhere safe?"

"Yes," Emelia confirmed, unwavering. "Do what you must."

Naomi curled her fingers in and out, feeling her powers coming to the surface. "Your house is going to be very soggy."

"Do it," Emelia said with force. "You know something I don't."

Facing the sea, Naomi studied the movements of the waves. She imagined the sea foam breaking and bubbling, the sand rippling underneath, shifting from the water's power.

Be a monster, she commanded. *Flood the shore and overtake the house.*

The sound of a pounding rainstorm exploded from the sea. The waves rose like wings of a monstrous beast. They pummeled the shore and thundered toward the house. Creaking and groaning echoed into the hillsides as the house's frame felt the impact.

Naomi turned away and placed a hand on Emelia's arm. "I'm sorry."

"Don't be." Emelia took a step away from the house, down the other side of the hill. "That house held hurtful memories anyway."

Naomi and Hux followed Emelia into the darkness of knee-high grass and mosquitos.

"So it was Estell," Hux mumbled.

Naomi shoved grass aside. "Yes. And Saul. But it was only them. They had no other Riders."

Hux moved quicker now, perhaps feeling the possibility of Saul and Estell at their backs.

Naomi felt the same. Being swallowed by the ground apparently hadn't killed Estell. Maybe Estell could survive the sea, too.

Emelia cut right, then stopped. "I'm off this way. You two keep going straight. It will lead you through town and back out into the east mountains."

"What can we say?" Naomi shrugged, at a loss. "We owe you so much."

"You owe me nothing," she said. "Do you know why I'm a widow?"

Naomi shook her head.

Emelia stepped closer to her again. "Because my husband, whom I loved very much, was taken by Calamity." She snapped her fingers. "Gone. All that was left was his shadow."

"His shadow?" Hux asked, slightly mortified.

"Yes. I woke to find his shadow lying next to me in bed. That's how I knew he hadn't run off."

Naomi swallowed away nausea. "Does his shadow still linger?"

"No." Emelia sounded relieved. "I swept it out the back door into a stormy night to be blown away with the wind. I won't let The Dark Hand haunt me like that."

"Why would Calamity only take your husband?" Hux wondered. "Why do you suppose you were spared?"

Emelia's eyes dimmed. "I loved my husband, but he wasn't afraid of the dark like I was. It intrigued him, and in the end, I believe his curiosity got the best of him. I, on the other hand, have no interest in the dark. The Dark Hand must have seen that in me and claimed an easier target."

The wind gusted and specks of salt water blew through the air.

Hux signaled onward with a tilt of his head. "We're losing time."

Naomi gave Emelia a quick hug before they parted.

As Emelia disappeared into the rolling hills, Naomi and Hux took off again toward town. They ran side by side, not speaking. The hills flattened slightly and a dirt trail appeared, weaving into town. All the buildings were dark. The only light came from the street torches. But the torches illuminated the dusty streets enough for Naomi to notice three bodies lying near the hooves of three antsy horses. The horses were tied to a fence outside of the tavern, trying to tug free. With one glance, Naomi knew they were royal horses. They were muscular and had short manes. Which meant the bodies lying in the dirt were Riders.

Naomi tore away from Hux's side and sprinted to them.

He followed, not even attempting to stop her.

"They're injured." She gasped and dropped down. When she placed her hand on the first man's shoulder and rolled him over, she saw blood seeping through his shirt at his ribs. A knife wound. And it had killed him.

Hux examined the second Rider and confirmed the same thing. "Saul has turned on his own."

"It's because he's Estell's puppet now." Naomi moved to the last Rider. "Or rather, he's Calamity's disciple."

The third Rider swung his arm up and grabbed Naomi's bicep. She jumped backward, startled at his movement.

"Release her!" Hux shouted. He reached for the Rider's fingers but stopped when the Rider spoke.

"Massoud," the Rider sputtered, clearly struggling to survive through his own knife wound.

Naomi hesitated, then nodded, staring down at the man who was so close to death.

With another shaking breath, the Rider whispered, "More on your side than you know."

She kept her focus on his fading eyes through her hair that fell over her shoulders and onto his chest. "Who's on my side?" she begged. "Tell me."

"More than you know," he said again, gasping. "The witch took our man."

"I know." Naomi squeezed her eyes shut, understanding the Rider's feeling of betrayal.

"But you—" He coughed and blood came from his mouth. "You have—" Another cough. "Allies."

The Riders head thunked back to the ground and his chest stopped moving. When his eyes turned gray, Naomi hung her head and pressed her hands against his wound. She didn't know this man, but that didn't matter. He had died believing in her.

"Oh, please spare him," Naomi prayed. Her shaking hands covered his wound as she begged with nature. *Heal him. Give him life again.*

Something soft tickled her palms and she looked down, hopeful. A patch of white flowers and bright green grass had sprouted from the knife wound, but the Rider remained unmoving. Naomi had the power to control nature. And from the looks of it, she had the power to somehow create bits of nature. But she wasn't a healer.

Hux put his hand on Naomi's shoulder. "You can't save everyone. This isn't your fault."

She rose, still trembling. "Saul and Estell won't stop. The

ocean may have slowed them down, but even the ground couldn't swallow up that golden witch."

"So we move onward to find Ferrin and Vira," Hux ordered as he began to loosen one of the horse's ropes from the fence.

Naomi watched him. "If we head off with one of their horses, Saul will know what to look for when he pursues us."

Hux shoved the rope in her hands. "So we ride faster than him."

CHAPTER SEVEN

Ferrin woke from his shared dream with Naomi and knew it was time to go. Seeing Naomi's face in Tal's cathedral gave him a rush of adrenaline. He needed to get to her. Something was standing next to her. Some*one*. A face he couldn't make out. Not because the person was hiding in the shadows, but because the face was blurred. As if the dream couldn't decide whether or not the face was there. It felt menacing to him, like the being lurked over Naomi's shoulder, waiting to pounce. And yet it was only a dream. Not everything in his prophesied dreams were true. But he couldn't take the chance. The dream was recurring, and that meant something.

Ferrin pulled open his door to reveal the Draycott Inn's hallway. It was dark and frigid, the wall's oil lamps flickering. As he stepped out, a shadow swept up the wall. He hesitated. Moving his arm, he watched his own shadow glide along the wall like a slender tree branch. The shadow he just saw hadn't been his own.

He rushed to Vira's door and knocked. When she opened the door, she was dressed in day clothes and her normally poised eyes were distraught.

He frowned. "What's wrong?"

She shoved the door open all the way. "You come knocking on my door and you ask *me* what's wrong?"

"You look off," he interrogated.

"I can't find Millie."

"It's the middle of the night and she is gone?"

"Exactly." Vira wrapped her cloak tighter around her arms and stepped out into the hallway. "She should be sleeping right next to me, yet she's not."

"I saw a shadow," Ferrin said quickly. "A moment ago."

"Show me."

Ferrin pointed down the hallway toward the stairs that led down to the tavern.

They strode side by side, fast and quiet.

"Why are you awake?" Vira asked, as they descended the stairs.

"Because I know where Naomi and Hux are."

Vira stopped short at the bottom of the stairway. "How?"

"Naomi and I shared the same dream again. The one of Tal being killed and Calamity entering the cathedral." He smiled a fraction. "In our dream, I talked to her. They're in Blaire, but I told her to leave and we would meet them halfway between here and there."

A crash came from the tavern, pulling their attention away from one another.

Ferrin lifted a hand out of reflex, ready to send a wave of energy toward whoever was lurking about.

Vira lowered his arm when she saw the person rise up from the ground. It was Millie. Her hair a mess and a pot in hand.

"What are you doing, love?" Vira moved toward her daughter but stopped when Millie looked at her.

Millie's eyes were dark. Expressionless. Blank.

The look struck Ferrin's core. This wasn't the Millie he

knew. This wasn't the kind, eager, excited little girl he had kept watch over for a month. She was something different now. A shell of a person.

"Millie," Vira barked.

"Don't," Millie rasped. She held up the pot and shook it. "I almost had him and you ruined it."

Vira took another step toward her. "Millie! Wake up!"

"I am awake, witch! Do you think I could have caught that rat while sleeping?"

"What rat?" Vira whispered. "Millie. Please."

A sudden disturbance in Ferrin's spirit told him to act. He pushed past Vira and grabbed the little girl's shoulders. "Millie! Step out of the dark!"

The pot fell from her hand as she attempted to rip away from him. "I'm safe here!" she screamed.

"No, you're not!" He gave her one hard shake. "Millicent, daughter of Vira, WAKE UP!"

Millie's pupils shrank to their normal size and her muscles relaxed. She was suddenly limp in Ferrin's grasp, looking at him with furrowed brows. "Ferrin?" she said, unsure.

He nodded, clenching his teeth. "Tell me why you're down here in the tavern."

Millie glanced over his shoulder at Vira. "I don't know."

Vira stepped up to Ferrin's shoulder and placed a hand on Millie's face. "Love, are you alright?"

"I'm fine, Mum, but why am I down here?"

Ferrin looked over at Vira, fear clinging to his eyes. "The Dark Hand. It's acting on her."

Vira covered her mouth, shaking her head.

Millicent's round eyes focused on Ferrin. "Calamity?" Her voice swung with panic. "I'm going to die?"

"No." He wrapped his arms around her, holding her close and secure. "Calamity will not have you."

"Graves," Vira said through a shaky breath. She put her hand on Ferrin's shoulder and bowed her head. "She has to come with us."

"I know."

Millicent looked up at her mother. "You're not going to leave me this time?"

Tears threatened to escape, but Vira kept them back. "I'm not going to leave you. You're coming with us."

A skittering noise came from under the bar stools and a damp rat scampered across the floor and disappeared again under the door.

Ferrin cast a glance its way, swallowing a gag at the thought of Millie trying to capture it with a kitchen pot. As if Calamity couldn't help itself but to hunt down the filthiest creature in the city.

"The horses are fed and rested," he said. "Let's move. There is no reason to wait for light."

"You know where to find Naomi?" Vira asked, shoving apples from the table under her cloak.

Ferrin patted his chest, feeling the quill under his shirt and against his heart. "I'll always know where to find her."

CHAPTER EIGHT

One minute Naomi was riding behind Hux on their stolen Le'Garian horse, and the next she was flat on her back, on the ground, Hux lying on top of her. For a moment she thought the horse had thrown them off, but the birds were screaming and the sound of rocks clacking against each other sounded throughout the mountain. Naomi looked around frantically, noticing how the trees looked parallel to the ground. Suddenly the ground felt like it was moving and Hux rolled off of her.

Then she was flipping again, rolling to her feet, yet somehow still falling, until a thud that jerked her vision sent the world to a screeching halt. The trees were upright again and she lay on her back, staring up at the sky.

The horse scrambled up and skittered away, making small clicking noises and pawing at the ground.

"Am I dreaming?" Naomi shouted over the sound of the disturbed forest creatures.

Hux sat up, frozen stiff. He held his arms out in front of him, examining them, as if trying to determine whether or not he was real.

"Hux!" Naomi boomed. She pushed herself up and leaned toward him to jab him in the shoulder. "Am I awake?"

"You're awake." He turned to look at her. "Thãen. It—it tipped."

Naomi shook her head, her stomach roiling all over again at what just happened. "No. No, it couldn't have. Calamity can't be winning."

"It's winning," Hux whispered. "We're starting to shift. Protection is losing us."

"No," she snapped. "It won't lose us. There is a way out of this!" She stood, pacing the dirt ground that had been tilled from the tip. "There is a way out of this, Hux. I am the way out of this." She drove her finger into her chest. "If I can't stop this, what is my bloodline for? What is the quill for? The necklace?"

Hux rose to steady legs. "You and everyone else think Protection will succeed. What makes you think that? What makes you ignore logic?"

"What? You still doubt? After all this?"

"After all of what?" he said hotly. "After we have been pursued day in and day out by Riders and a wicked golden witch? After Vira was shot with a deadly arrow? After the entire world just tipped?" His chin dropped to his chest, eyes shut. "I've tried so hard. I really have. I've tried not to doubt. But we're failing, Omi. That's it. The supreme beings are warring, and we're caught in the middle of it. One of them has to come out on top, and it may not be the god we want."

Naomi frowned, too stunned to speak. He couldn't be serious. "Wait until you hug Vira again," she dared. "You'll see Protection's hand then. You'll see how it plucked her from death."

A shadow fell over Hux's eyes. "Vira's survival was Ferrin's doing."

"And you think Ferrin finding me in the first place was a coincidence?" she challenged.

"I—" He looked down. "What are you saying?"

"Protection knew. It sees what we can't. It gave us who we needed." She played with the necklace between her collar bones. "I think it knew, centuries ago, about what would be happening today. That's why it put a plan in place. It created a way for us to end this."

He nodded, following. "You think Protection has a plan laid out that you must unravel?"

"It's the only thing that makes sense," she admitted, half defeated, half sure. "There is a pathway, we just need to find it."

CHAPTER NINE

When Le'Gar experienced Thãen tip, the gargoyles cried out. Their wings opened up as if to steady themselves, but they remained rooted to their buildings, even when the buildings were horizontal. When the stone city thudded back to its upright position, the stone creatures were safe, though rattled. But not every Le'Garian was so lucky. There were bodies in the streets. Those who had fallen from their windows or had been crushed by one of the tall ships that careened onto shore, free falling with the leaning terrain. The entire city was wet from the rush of water from the Desarian Sea that had smashed into the buildings before receding once again.

Eli ran through the streets, screams echoing around him. Bed linens, upturned market carts, books, glass bottles, shoes, loaves of bread, it all littered the ground. It looked as if Le'Gar had been chewed up and spit back out. The screams of its people penetrated into Eli's mind with much force, causing him to clench his teeth and dig his fingernails into his palms. He saw past their screams and into their innermost thoughts. The thoughts were riddled with fear and defeat, but hysteria was the emotion that he picked up on the most. Thãen's tip was a sickening blow. A horrific piece of evidence that The Hand of Calamity was gaining enough people to outweigh the balance of those who remained faithful to Protection.

"Ferrin, I need you to hear me," Eli whispered into the air. "Bring Naomi Massoud back to Le'Gar. The answer lies here."

A woman bumped into Eli's shoulder before moving on to race through the streets. He watched her go, feeling loss in her heart. She had lost someone in all this. The pain that Calamity was inflicting on the world sat heavy on his heart, now more than ever, and he picked up his pace, sprinting now. Well, sprinting as fast as an old man could.

The library building peaked above the city ahead. Eli knew Deirdre had been inside when the tip happened. He was on his way to meet her when the street was suddenly parallel with his falling body. It didn't take the mind of a Magnificent to figure out how dangerous a tipping library could be. Shelves don't hold books when they're leaning. They spill, and books aren't light.

Eli sprang up the stone steps two at a time, to the double wood doors of the library. He pushed them open and ran inside. The four-story rectangular building was littered with literature. Pages and hard covers lay splayed about like fresh snow. A mirror of Le'Gar's streets.

Eli cupped his hands around his mouth and shouted, "Deirdre!"

There was no answer, but he began to climb over the piles of books to get to the back of the building. Three stories of railings towered above him and he glanced up, half expecting to see Deirdre hanging from one for dear life. But the room was quiet.

Then a square trap door in the library's ground slammed open, sending books sailing.

Deirdre's head appeared from the ground, the rest of her hidden in the space that the door covered.

Eli ran to her, kicking books aside. "Are you hurt?"

"I'm not," she said, but a fresh cut sat above her eyebrow and swelling rested on her cheek.

"Were you down there when the tip happened?" Eli reached her and lowered his hand to help her out.

"Yes." She avoided his hand. "Come with me."

He sat on the ledge of the opening. His feet hung down and touched a set of stone steps. The way was dark, and though he was a Magnificent, his eyes had aged.

"I need your hand," he admitted.

Deirdre helped him in and led him down into the darkness. He kept his hand on her arm, trusting her to keep him steady. When they reached the bottom of the stairs, the walkway was narrow and damp. Eli stepped on roots that had protruded through the stone. He focused on each step, attempting to avoid a spill. Beneath his grip, Deirdre's arm grew rigid, mimicking the feel of stone. By now Eli was used to the sudden shifts that would happen to Deirdre's body. Though she walked about Le'Gar as a human, she was just as much a gargoyle as the ones that sat perched against the sky. When she could rest and be less on guard, she morphed into complete stone. A gray angle. Though Eli had lived for over 200 years, Deirdre was ancient even to him. She dated back to the moment The Hand of Protection found Thãen.

The tunnel cut right and ended at a ledge where an underground river flowed. The stone ledge along the rushing water was wide enough for Deirdre and Eli to inch along, which is what they did. Deirdre moved Eli's hand to her shoulder and took him forward. Her collarbone crunched under his fingertips as her stone form gradually shifted back to flesh and bone.

Deirdre broke the silence. "Here."

She teetered around the ledge where the river bent, and they came to a wide platform of stone that hung out over the slow-moving water. The rock walls surrounding the cove had hundreds of carved-out holes, which were meant to hold stacks of scrolls. Eli could tell because the ground was littered with them, soggy, and destroyed. Some were even plastered against the walls, as if they had fallen in the river and been thrown back out when Thãen had righted itself again. But one space in the wall still held a scroll. As if the scroll hadn't shifted when the world tipped.

That was the scroll Deirdre walked over to and pulled out. She handled it gingerly, slowly unrolling it. "All of these scrolls were important," she revealed. "Some of them date back to the creation of golden witches and Magnificents."

Eli pinched the bridge of his nose, attempting to, once again, wrap his mind around just how ancient Deirdre was. She had been living in Thãen when The Hand of Protection found their world. *That's* how many years she had lived.

"Did Protection direct you to keep these scrolls?" he asked. "What are they?" He wasn't used to being in the dark when it came to knowledge, and it bothered him.

"I wasn't directed to keep them, but I began keeping records of anyone who showed signs of possessing power as soon as Protection gave me the task of being enchanter of the gargoyles."

"Why?"

"Because I knew that Protection had created a bloodline to fulfill its plan of one day saving our world. I took it upon myself to make sure that plan would succeed, and that meant knowing who was of the sacred bloodline."

Eli nodded, massaging the beard on his chin. Deirdre was the one who had placed the enchantment on the gargoyles. Not a golden witch, like the stories claimed, but Deirdre. Before The

Hand of Protection found Thãen, Thãen had floated freely in the Outer Void. Then Protection found it and saw how vulnerable the people of Thãen were. Only humans. No golden witches, no Magnificents. Even Deirdre was human then. A seventeen-year-old girl. Protection had created golden witches and Magnificents because Protection knew that Calamity would find Thãen, and if the people of Thãen had to face The Dark Hand without magic, they wouldn't have a chance to survive.

"What's that scroll?" Eli pointed to the unwrapped scroll in her hand. "It didn't fall."

"That's what I wanted to show you." She waved him toward her. "I want you to see what it holds."

He carefully stepped over soaking wet scrolls on his way to her side. When he reached her, he peered over her shoulder and his stomach knotted. The scroll looked to be a genealogy tree, but every name had been crossed out.

Except for the last one.

Naomi Massoud.

But right away Eli noticed the problem. None of the crossed-out names above hers were Massouds. In fact, they were all different surnames.

"This isn't the ancestry of the Massoud bloodline," he stated.

"I know." Deirdre exhaled and ran her finger over Naomi's name. "We don't need to look at an ancestry tree to know Naomi is the last descendant of the Massoud bloodline. I can show you that scroll if you'd like, but I believe you already know this about her."

"I can't lie, I'd love to see that scroll, but I fear it may be plastered against the rock or at the bottom of this river." He tilted his head at the mess of paper all around. "The world tipped, you know."

Deirdre's eyes fogged over for a moment as her stone self

fought to the surface, but she blinked it away and flicked a grin instead. "Joking at a time like this, Eli."

He grinned beneath his beard and nodded his chin back at the scroll. "So what is this, then?"

"This is a record I've written and kept. Of everyone who has bled black."

"Bled black?" Eli withdrew. "The only people who have bled the color black were found to be disciples of Calamity." He dropped his finger on the name directly above Naomi's. "Gregory Hai. I remember him. Found dead on the docks with black blood seeping from his ears. He was Calamity's disciple." He moved his finger up to the middle of the list. "Henrietta Laughlin. Caught stealing a child from its bed nearly one hundred years ago. Also Calamity's disciple." He paced, crossing his arms. "Why are they all crossed off? Dead?"

Deirdre nodded.

"Except for Naomi," he confirmed.

She nodded again.

Eli stopped pacing and faced her. "When did she bleed black?"

Deirdre fumbled over her words. "It was a vulnerable time for Naomi."

"Tell me," he demanded. "If she truly bled the color black, I must know."

"It wasn't long ago. She had been attacked in one of Le'Gar's streets. Her attacker didn't manage to accomplish what he was attempting, but Naomi still took a knife to the cheek." Deirdre steadied her breathing, her sorrow for Naomi showing through every feature of her face. "Naomi was hysterical when she burst into my library. It was incredibly early in the morning, after her lantern shift, and I had just arrived to begin my own shift at the library. When I saw her, I knew she had sought me out for help. The cut on her face was deep and needed sewing. So I did it myself."

"You didn't call for the doctor?" Eli interrogated.

"Not after I saw the color of her blood," she said softly. "She would have been killed."

Eli paced again, rubbing his eyes, chewing his lip. "Did Naomi say anything about the condition of her blood?"

Deirdre shook her head. "She never saw it. She was so shaken up and distracted with crying that I was able to toss the bandages and cloths away without her seeing. I was quick about it."

"Why?" Eli whispered. "Why does she bleed black? You said Protection had a hand in creating the Massoud bloodline. Why would she be a disciple of Calamity if her ancestry was created to fulfill a specific plan laid out by The Hand of Protection?"

"I don't know," Deirdre admitted with a whisper. "But she never acted out against Protection and I've never seen her step out of line in any way. She can't be a disciple."

"If not a disciple, then what?"

"I don't know," she said again. "But Mavelic sees her and knows her. She is not dangerous."

"Mavelic." Eli's spine stiffened. The name was like a rushing sigh in his ears. "You speak the ancient name of The Hand of Protection freely."

"Its name has been lost with the passing of time," Deirdre sounded sorry to say. "We have resorted to calling it something we can better comprehend. The Hand of Protection sounds more like something we can comprehend. But calling it by its real name? That gives it real power. Power we may be unwilling to submit to. Mavelic holds us, yes, but do we fully trust it won't let us fall? Do we trust it to have total power over us?"

"And what would happen if we started calling it Mavelic again?"

Deirdre looked down at Naomi's name. "I don't know. But when I say it, I feel a power well up in my chest. Like it means something. When I say the name, it stirs me." She pointed upward. "It stirs the gargoyles. They feel it, too."

He nodded. "Does it feel to you that we are getting closer to discovering how Naomi can save our world? Are we making progress?" With a desperate sigh, he willed, once again, for Ferrin to show up in Le'Gar with Naomi Massoud at his side. "When you first told me your story, you mentioned a key that would set Protection's plan in motion."

"There is a key," Deirdre confirmed. "It's the golden quill. But I was not given the knowledge about how to use the quill. Though Mavelic took my human body and transformed me to be like the gargoyles, therefore granting me morality, it didn't grant me full knowledge. I work for Protection, yes, but I don't know all. I only know this." She stood straighter, clenching the scroll. "The quill can only be used once, so when we figure out how to use it, we must do it correctly the first time. Or Mavelic's plan, whatever it is, will come to nothing."

CHAPTER TEN

When Naomi saw what was supposed to be the tent town of Zul, she leapt off her horse and began to run.

Hux nudged the horse into a canter, following her, seeing the same thing she did. From the east mountains, they had a perfect view of the town below.

Or what was left of it.

Naomi thrashed down the mountainside, breathing heavy, swallowing tears.

"No," she sobbed. "Please, no."

"Naomi!" Hux shouted behind her.

But she kept running. The village of tents where she had first met Vira and Hux was burnt to a crisp. Nothing remained standing. And perhaps Naomi would have thought it had been pillaged if it weren't for the mark left scorched in the ground.

A black handprint the size of the entire village.

The ravine was dry. The people were gone.

By the time Naomi reached the outline of the handprint, sweat poured down her face and her lungs threatened to explode. She surveyed the destruction, hoping to see movement. Hoping to spot any survivors. But there was no one. Only a ghostly wind that sent ashes swirling into the air.

Hux reined his horse to a halt and jumped to the ground. "Omi." He charged for her and took her arm. "Think clearly. Calamity may still be here."

She continued to look around, gasping for air. Truly nothing stood. The ashen debris sat in mounds, like rolling hills.

"It's not still here," she spat. "There is nothing left to take!"

Hux let her arm go, allowing himself to take in the scene of death around him.

"Where will Calamity hit next?" she wailed. "Le'Gar? Raina? What's it waiting for?"

"It's waiting for you, Naomi," Hux thundered. "It's looking for you. So pull back. We're out in the open."

A movement came from the base of the west mountains, where the treeline butted up to the burnt land. There was a flicker of black, and then it was gone, hidden behind a mound of ash that lay a few yards ahead.

Naomi took off in a sprint.

"Naomi!" Hux hollered.

Again, she ignored him. She pumped her arms, tearing through piles of black dust toward the west mountains. Inwardly, she searched for a piece of nature to control. There was nothing. Everything around her was dead. The soil beneath the ash felt far away, almost unreachable. But she dug deeper.

Rise up, she demanded. *Swallow the ash.*

The ground beneath her quivered as she ran. She was nearing the west mountains and once again she saw a dark figure dash from behind one hill of ash to the next.

She quickened, launching herself into overdrive. Her legs felt weightless. The ground barely met her feet.

Rise up! she screamed at the soil. *Stop my prey.*

A tornado of soil burst up from the ground, spiraling like a spinning thorn. It tore across the burnt terrain and collided with a pile of ash, creating a massive gray cloud of particles. The figure hiding behind the pile was now exposed, coughing in the thick, soiled air. It lifted its arm and sent a wave of energy rippling across the air. The wave hit Naomi square in the chest and she stumbled, falling to her knees.

Capture its feet in the ground, she thought.

The figure made an attempt to leap her way, but the ground suctioned the figure's boots.

Naomi pushed herself to her feet and charged into the thinning cloud of ash and dirt. She swiped her hair out of her face and withdrew the sword at her side.

"Who are you?" she shouted. "Tell me now!"

The dust had settled, and her target was frozen five feet in front of her. He lifted both of his hands, his black shirt covered in filth and his hair caked with ash.

"Naomi," he spoke through short breaths. "For graves' sake, it's me."

Her arms fell to her sides, shaking uncontrollably. The sword in her hand clattered to the ground and the soil released her prisoner.

"Ferrin." Her voice crumbled.

He took two sturdy steps toward her, but she was faster. She careened into his half-open arms, slamming into his chest and strangling him with a hug. The feel of his hair against her cheek and even the smell of his sweat made Naomi hold onto him even longer.

"Graves, Naomi," he mumbled into her shoulder. "When did you get so powerful?"

She felt him smile into her skin and she dreaded ever having to pull away, but she grabbed his arms and backed up to face him.

"Are you okay?" she whispered.

His voice came out just as soft. "I'm fine. So is Vira."

"Thank Protection. You have the quill?" she asked, hopeful.

"I do." He patted his chest. "Under here. Its glow faded after you left."

"So did the necklace."

Naomi grabbed the pendant at her chest. When she glanced down, she saw it glowed softly with light again, like a star.

Ferrin's mouth ticked upward. "The lock has been reunited with the key."

Dirt sprayed the back of Naomi's legs as Hux and his horse finally caught up, skidding to a stop.

"You better be thankful Naomi realized it was you," Hux exclaimed, as he dropped to the ground. "I thought she was going to kill whomever she was after."

Naomi scowled, but a smile hid behind her eyes. Hux was right. In that moment, she had the urge to demolish anything that stood in her way. She had power now, and she wanted to use it. If Calamity could destroy entire villages, she could do one better. She could destroy *it*. And she vowed that she would.

Hux searched the foothills. "Where is she?"

"She's fine, my friend." Ferrin squeezed Hux's shoulder in greeting. "She's in the cover of the mountains with Millicent."

Naomi sucked in a gasp. "You brought Millicent?"

Ferrin nodded. "Calamity tried to take her. She's safest with us."

"But we don't know what we're walking into," Naomi argued. "I don't know what's waiting for us in Le'Gar."

"Le'Gar?" He crossed his arms and faced her squarely. "You want to go back?"

Naomi nodded, staring up at him. "There is something for me there. Nature told me."

He studied her, watching the surety behind her expression. When she had left him in Mira Isla, she still had a look of uneasiness, like she was still doubting herself and afraid of fully stepping into her power. Now, after watching her draw a sword on him and seeing nature listen to her like she was their army commander, he realized she owned her power and had crossed over the line. And in the right direction, too.

With a gentle hand, Ferrin lifted her hair from her shoulder and brushed it behind her back. She froze under his touch. Her heart wailed and she was unable to conjure up words. But Hux cleared his throat and pointed toward the west mountains.

To Le'Gar," he offered, keeping his gaze away from the two.

Naomi stepped away from Ferrin and nodded. "Yes, we must."

Ferrin brushed by her and began the trek across the foothills. Hux stepped up next to her and gave her a silent, devious raise of his eyebrows. Naomi scowled again, warding off his teasing. But she couldn't help but know exactly what he was teasing her about.

As they ascended into the west mountains, spits of rain began to fall. Zul's ruins disappeared behind them and trees with fresh, new, spring foliage surrounded them instead. Naomi breathed in the smell of damp forestry and even welcomed the small bits of rain that splotched against her skin. Anything was better than a ghost town of ashes.

When the forest grew thicker, Ferrin weaved off to the left and called out. "It's us, Vira. I found them."

From behind the wide trunk of a kauri tree, Vira's black horse shifted into view. She sat on top, her green eyes just as vibrant as Naomi remembered. It was as if she had never been pierced by an arrow. She had the same look of intensity as the first time Naomi met her. Only now she seemed to hold an extra protectiveness, because a small girl sat behind her.

"Hi, Naomi!" the girl just about cheered. "Isn't this cool? I'm here, too!"

"Very cool," Naomi lied through a smile. "You must have run very fast like I told you to the last time I saw you." She swallowed, putting the memory away again. "Good job."

Millicent held a thumb up, grinning.

Vira chuckled then dismounted, signaling for Millie to stay put. She stepped toward Naomi then pressed her hands together as if to pray. "Thank you. You kept my daughter safe in Mira Isla and I am extremely grateful."

Naomi reached out and took ahold of Vira's hands. "It's good to see you, Vira. You kept *me* safe that night." She looked Vira in the eyes and tried to relay just how grateful she was. Vira had placed herself in-between Naomi and a lethal arrow, taking the hit from the arrow and nearly losing her life. Vira truly risked her life to save Naomi, and Naomi would do the same for her.

Vira squeezed Naomi's hands. "You've been practicing your power."

Naomi frowned. "Yes. Hux and I have been training with swords, and I'm feeling nature more organically. I have more control. How could you tell?"

"I feel your energy. You truly are getting stronger. Well done, Naomi. Are you ready to keep emerging?"

Her words ignited something in Naomi's stomach. *Emerging.* As if she were a butterfly coming out of a cocoon, not an explosion of unknowns. Not a threat.

"I'm ready," she answered. "I think I'm almost there."

Vira stepped back. "Good. We will be needing you." Finally, she looked past Naomi to Hux.

Hux had been standing still and quiet, taking in the sight of his oldest friend. The friend he thought he had lost.

"So you've been teaching her how to sword fight," Vira said, pleased. "I'm sure you gave her a difficult time, knowing your skill."

He didn't say anything, just waited for her to walk his way. When she stood in front of him, he didn't throw himself into her or offer a hand. He merely squared his shoulders, matching her height.

Vira set a hand on his cheek, watching him stand steady like he always did. Under every circumstance he was a stoic beast, never overreacting, never acting impulsively. But he had been different on the day the arrow had struck her. Though she had been nearly unconscious, she still heard him, and she remembered it now.

Please don't leave us yet, he had whispered in her ear as she lay dying under Ferrin's hands. *Please breathe. Please, Vira. It's going to kill me if I lose you for good. Please.*

"I heard you," Vira tried to speak only to him.

He blinked, still unmoving.

She smiled and ran her thumb gently across his cheek. "I'm still here."

A weak-lipped smile arched beneath his scruff. "And thank Protection that you are. I thank Protection for putting you in Ferrin's hands."

"You can see Protection at work now?" Her question came out surprised.

"Sometimes I do." His strong hand found hers, holding it against his cheek. "Often times I doubt, but I'm learning to believe."

"So I see you've grown, too," she said, watching his eyes a moment longer.

The rain picked up and the bottoms of the leaves flipped up as a gust of wind blew through.

Ferrin looked up at the canopy overhead. "We have miles of forestry above us and only clover at our feet. No caves. No alcoves." He sighed. "No shelter."

Naomi nudged into him, already calmer than she had been in a month. "Do we have a plan?"

"You said we're off to Le'Gar," he said, matter-of-fact. "You feel that's where we need to go."

"I was told," she corrected. "By nature."

"I was told to return to Le'Gar as well, though not by nature," he revealed. "But I'll tell you about that once we stop to rest. Right now, we need to keep moving. I feel someone at our backs."

"It's Estell," Naomi said. "We saw her. Her and Saul."

Ferrin stared deeper into the mountainside. "Yeah. That's what I was afraid of. I knew nature couldn't keep her down."

CHAPTER ELEVEN

The rain didn't let up. It only fell harder. Naomi sat behind Ferrin on his horse, burying her face in his cloak to shield herself from the water, but it was no use. Her lips trembled from the chill and her fingers were pruned. They moved forward but seemed to make no progress. Perhaps it was because night had fallen, and it was difficult to judge distance in the dark. Or maybe how cold she felt was at the forefront of her mind and time was just a second thought. Springtime or not, she was freezing, and she wished with every passing second that the gray peaks of Le'Gar would spike through the trees up ahead and offer them a roof over their heads. But Le'Gar never came. Zul was days away from the city and its gargoyles. No matter how long she and the others had been traveling, it hadn't been long enough.

Ferrin reached around and placed a hand on Naomi's shivering thigh. "Are you doing alright?"

"I think it's safe to say I'm cold," she sputtered.

"Vira!" Ferrin called ahead.

In the rain, Vira and Millicent were nearly invisible on their own horse. The only reason Naomi could see Hux and his steed was because he was right next to her and Ferrin.

"Are you ready to stop?" Vira sounded hopeful. "I think Millie's done in."

"Pull to the right," Ferrin directed.

"No," Naomi said.

Ferrin leaned back to her. "No?"

Naomi searched the air and soil. She could hear small sighs escaping the surrounding woods, happy to be taking in such heavy rain. But the sighs grew louder farther ahead. The sound of larger trees. Ones with wider leaves that could create more of a barrier from the rain.

"Up ahead," Naomi called to Vira. "There's better cover. And I can get us more."

Vira nudged her horse onward at a quicker rate.

Ferrin shook water from his hair and spoke over his shoulder. "Why didn't you just say so in the first place?"

Naomi shrugged and sniffled. "I'm not in charge."

"Come on, Omi," he grunted, leaning forward to push his horse faster. "Step on our toes. Get in our way. You're a leader, too."

A flip caught her stomach. *Omi.* The name he had once refused to use.

"Oh, I'll step on your toes," she jokingly threatened. "If you get in my way, ranger."

He huffed. "I wouldn't dream of it."

"Here," she demanded, looking up. "Stop here."

Whereas the live oaks and pine trees gave sparse protection, the kapok trees here were broad and bushy, creating a barrier above the maple trees which sat lower. Double protection, Naomi realized. And after she mentally ordered the maple trees to spread their leaves wide to eliminate space for the rain to pass, they had a decently dry place to rest under the branches.

The horses eventually lay down near each other, feeling for the warmth of the other. Though the maples blocked out most of the water, drops still fell through to the already soaked moss and clover. It was useless to start a fire, but just sitting under a mildly dry dome of trees was better than the last few hours. For the first time since the group had been reunited, they sat huddled, facing each other. And they faced the question that had been on their minds since the night of Mira Isla's invasion.

Ferrin pulled out the golden feather from beneath his shirt. The haze that shone off of the quill was once again as bright as the moon. Light from it reflected on his face, revealing his mossy-colored eyes. "What happens when the quill and the necklace touch?"

Naomi sat beside him and offered him an open hand. "Here. I'll show you."

Across from her, Millicent sat in Vira's lap, leaning into her mother's chest, almost asleep. But the girl sat up, bright eyed, when Naomi took both items, one in each hand.

Hux sat between Vira and Naomi and he placed his hand on Naomi's arm. "Wait."

Naomi looked at him, the quill in her left hand, the necklace in her right. "It's alright. I've done it before."

"And nothing dangerous happened?"

"Nothing dangerous," she confirmed. "It only gave me answers."

Hux withdrew his hand and sat back, nodding at her to continue.

Naomi raised the items in front of her face. She held the necklace by the sides of the pendant, securing the pearl between her fingertips. Aiming the tip of the quill at the pearl, she let them touch. When they did, the pearl burst with even greater light and began to swirl, like a thick fog was trapped inside. The substance morphed outside of the pearl and onto the quill, filling the quill's tip with light in the same way a normal quill would hold ink. The golden feather glimmered like melted coin as the tip sat ready to be used. Ready to be written with.

"The pearl holds the ink," Vira marveled, holding a hand to her chest. "It truly does."

A pulse of energy wove up Naomi's arm as she held onto the quill, as if the light itself itched to be released in the form of writing.

"Well?" Ferrin whispered. His stare never moved from the marvelous golden feather. "Are you going to write with it?"

Naomi's heart beat in triple time. "Where?"

"Anywhere." He rolled up his sleeve to reveal his forearm and thrusted it toward her. "Here."

She drew back. "You think I'm going to use the quill on you? I don't even know how it works. I'm not risking that."

Dropping the necklace into the breast of her shirt, she used her now free hand to roll up her own sleeve.

Ferrin grabbed her wrist as she brought the quill toward her skin and stopped her inches away.

"Are you mad?" he spat. "So it was foolish of me to suggest testing the quill on myself but you thought you could do the same? I'll say it again: Are you *mad*?"

"Graves, Omi, he's right." Hux bellowed. "What are you thinking?"

Naomi clenched her teeth and her nose flared. She threw a glare at Ferrin, his hand still wrapped around her wrist. Thunder echoed in the distance.

"You told me to step on your toes," she reminded him through angry breaths. "But you won't let me."

His grip loosened as his face did, too. "I didn't say that you should put yourself in danger. Sometimes a leader can take too big risks, and it hurts them rather than benefits those they lead." With gentler fingers, he lowered her hand to the clover, the quill still in her grasp. "Let's not try writing with the quill on any of us, alright? Try writing with it on my cloak?"

She watched as he placed her hand down. Scars covered the tops of his hands and, now that she was searching, she noticed them on his exposed forearm too.

"Fine," she gave in. "I'll try it on your cloak."

The rain outside of the protection of the tree blew sideways, but with a lift of his hand, Ferrin cast a weak wall of energy behind him, blocking any rain from entering their dry spot. The wind seemed to respond in irritation, blowing harder at the circle of travelers.

Naomi bent toward Ferrin and pulled the edge of his cloak in her lap. All four faces around her glowed with anticipation as she lowered the quill to the material. She held the quill like she would if she were writing and let the tip touch the cloak. Sucking in a breath, she drew gentle loops, a simple doodle. But nothing came from the quill. The shimmering ink remained fixed to the tip of the feather and refused to leave behind any trace on the cloak.

Hux sat back. "That's odd."

"Not what the quill is looking for," Ferrin said.

Naomi held the quill in her hands again, like it was a fragile bird. "We need paper."

"Perhaps," Ferrin agreed. "Or something entirely different."

Millicent leaned forward from Vira's lap. "How does the ink get back into the necklace?" she asked.

Naomi reached into the top of her shirt and down to her breasts, where she had dropped the necklace. She pulled it out and held it up, revealing its glow.

"It never runs dry," she explained. "It's like an everlasting source."

"Bizarre," Vira marveled. "Unlike anything I've ever seen."

Naomi clasped the necklace around her neck again and handed the quill back to Ferrin. He didn't accept it right away.

"I think maybe you should hold onto it," he suggested.

"I don't want to," she argued. Then her eyes fell. "I don't want to carry all the weight myself. It feels like a lot."

He nodded, understanding. "Okay."

He took the quill and placed it back under his shirt and against his chest. She smiled in thanks and he returned the look.

"So Le'Gar," Vira nudged at the hovering question. "Why go back? What's there?" She tilted her chin at Ferrin across the circle. "You've been saying the same thing, that you feel we need to get Naomi back to Le'Gar."

Naomi looked at him. "Yes, who told you to return to Le'Gar?"

He leaned back on his hands. In the dark now, without the glow of the quill to light up the space, his features blended with the night, which gave Naomi more of a chance to study him without feeling like he was watching her just as intently.

Ferrin's voice took over the darkness. "Eli has called out to me."

Naomi perked up. "Old Man Magnificent?"

"Yes. He's been sending messages out into the wind for me to hear." Ferrin tipped his chin at her. "You're needed in Le'Gar. He sounds desperate, like he knows something we don't."

"But you sounded surprised when I said I wanted to go back to Le'Gar," she pointed out. "Yet you've felt the same all along."

"I wasn't surprised that you wanted to go, but that you also knew we must return. I want you to return to Le'Gar because I think the answers do lie there, but you can make your own decisions. I would never force you into danger by making you go back to Le'Gar." His gaze trailed away, his mind perhaps traveling back in time when he could not save Oliver Massoud from being killed by Estell. "King Tal works directly with Calamity. If you go back, you'll be walking right into the place that wants you dead the most. You understand that, right?"

Both Hux and Vira were watching her, waiting for her answer. None of them would force her to do something dangerous. She had to be the one to choose the direction of her life, and that realization sat heavy on her chest. A small part of her wanted to rely on them to tell her the next steps to take, but Vira could only have so many prophetic dreams, Hux could only teach her so many tricks with the sword, and Ferrin could only wield so much energy and heal so many bodies before his own body unraveled on itself. None of her companions were invincible, and none of them were truly responsible for her. Her decisions were hers, and what she decided to do next could bring harm to herself, but it could also mean saving Thãen from falling into Calamity's palm. She could save their world and keep it secure in the palm of Protection. She knew this was the path she was destined to take.

"I understand the weight of going back," she stated with firmness. "The danger. But there is no other option. If Le'Gar needs me, I'm going back. Back then, when I lived in Le'Gar and had no idea how powerful my name was, one of the gargoyles sacrificed itself to tell me to flee before King Tal could find me. I think, even though I didn't know it at the time, that the gargoyles have always kept watch over me. If I go back, I have no doubt they will protect me still. I have no army but the four of you. You're all powerful, but it's not enough. Maybe the gargoyles can help. It isn't far-fetched, is it, to think that stone beings can help?"

"It's not far-fetched in the slightest," Vira agreed. "We will just need to figure out how to release them." She held Millicent's head against her chest, now that she had finally dozed off. "We will continue on as we have been."

Naomi nodded toward the sleeping girl. "Will she be alright?"

Ferrin and Vira shared a look before Vira answered. "Yes. She is safest here with us. She will have to accept the challenging journey."

"She's capable," Ferrin sounded genuine. "And she wouldn't want Naomi to see her as weak." A little grin touched his lips.

"Me?" Naomi pointed to herself. "I'd never think she's weak."

"But she doesn't know that, and she looks up to you."

Noami turned his words over in her head, then swallowed. "But I took away her mom."

Vira lifted her eyes over Millicent's head to cast a sharp stare. "You didn't take me from her. *I* chose to look for you. And thank Protection I did, because now my daughter has the possibility of a life that doesn't involve a war with the gods. She could have a secure life in the palm of Protection. And just so the air is clear, you mean just as much to me as my own daughter does."

A full set of tears bobbed in Naomi's throat. "Thank you," she choked. "But you don't have to claim me as your own."

Vira stroked Millicent's hair. "We'd all claim you, Naomi. That's why we're all here. We believe in you and your powers. But don't forget this very important truth: you meant something even before you found your powers, and we care about that version of Naomi, too."

CHAPTER TWELVE

King Tal stumbled out of his bedroom, holding his robe closed at his chest. With bare feet, untamed hair, and nothing but his pajamas underneath, he knew he must look absolutely feral. But anxiety didn't care if it was the middle of the night or not. Anxiety struck when it wanted to, and it had pierced him awake.

The hall walls stretched tall with alcoves housing marble statues of past kings and queens that watched Tal as he brisked by. A stairway at the end of the hall went up on the right and down on the left. Both ways could eventually get Tal to the cathedral hall, but the left was more direct and the night guards may see him. Which didn't matter all that much, only that the King wasn't too fond of feeling as if he had to explain why he was up at such an hour and pacing around as if he were unraveling.

He chose the right staircase.

Weaving down halls, dodging the occasional night guard and three side staircases later, he finally stood outside the doors of the cathedral hall. One guard stood in front of the double doors and his eyebrows turned in when he saw the King.

"Sir?" the guard pried. "Are you well?"

"Well enough," Tal grunted. "Now let me through. I have something urgent to address."

The guard straightened. "Shall I summon the Riders or the Council?"

"No. In fact, don't let anyone know I'm here."

The guard stepped aside. "Yes, sir."

Tal brushed past the guard and into the expansive hall that leapt with shadows. The hanging lanterns had been lit, as they were each night, and they rocked slowly when a breeze swept through the cracks in the stone walls. With every step across the runner that led from the door to the throne, Tal's pulse quickened. But he kept his posture steady and his breathing even. He was still a disciple of Calamity, and he would play that game as long as he needed to, but if The Dark Hand caught on that Tal was faking his alliance, he would be killed. Just like what had happened to his father. He needed to keep Calamity believing that he was a faithful disciple.

Standing in front of his throne, he faced the crimson-red curtain that hung behind it. The curtain blocked anyone in the cathedral hall from seeing what sat behind. Tal had heard all the speculations. The rumors of what the curtain could be hiding. Even after hearing every speculation under the sun, he wished at least one of them were true. Anything was better than what the curtain truly covered up. Only this time, perhaps what lay behind the curtain would help him. If he played this right, it could.

With an angry arm, he threw aside the curtain and stepped through the split. It closed behind him, shutting him in the darkness. Nothing but stone walls and a stone floor.

And a golden basin atop a golden pedestal.

He stepped forward, as he had done so many times, and stared down at the basin. It was shallow, like a birdbath, but it didn't hold water. It held black liquid. Tal knew from experience that the liquid was thick like mercury and cold like steel. It had startled him the first time he used it, but his father promised him he would be fine. And his father had been right. Physically, he was always fine, but mentally—now that was another story.

King Tal pressed his fingertips together and brought them to his chin like a prayer. He shut his eyes and breathed in, digging for the right words. He needed to do this correctly. He needed to play the game.

"In the name of *Hilith*," he murmured. "Show me the girl's origin story so that I may ruin her."

Keeping his eyes shut, he bowed forward and plunged his head into the thick, black liquid.

His ears became mute and he could no longer sense his surroundings. When he opened his eyes, he stared down at a city, as if he were a bird in flight. The city he hovered over was pebbly, from its seashore to its streets. White domes were the dominating architecture, with the occasional wooden hut. Grassy plains filled with wildflowers sat at the city's back, while the sea crashed at its front.

Beezus.

King Tal knew of this territory. He had never been there, but he knew of someone who had. And that someone was Naomi Massoud. The girl who arrived in Le'Gar as Naomi Smyth. The girl who had lived as a Smyth until Tal ordered a search for anyone named Massoud. She had fled, exposing herself. It was a foolish thing to do, he thought, to flee when no one had even questioned her yet. But he didn't blame her. He had heard the stories of Oliver Massoud. A boy who jumped from the cathedral roof to end his own life. It was the story that everyone in Tal's family told.

But he knew the truth. After taking the position as king and taking orders from Calamity, he knew what had really happened to Oliver. It was not suicide, but murder. Had Naomi stayed in Le'Gar, he would have ordered the exact same thing to be done to her. That is, until his father died under Calamity's hand. His father didn't want to serve Calamity anymore. And his father didn't want Tal to, either. His father died in the middle of writing Tal a note. The note was cryptic and unfinished, but Tal knew the note was a guide on how to save Le'Gar and its people from Calamity's approaching doom.

Now, staring down at Beezus, the King watched a dark cloud roll in. The people of Beezus looked up, far enough away that Tal couldn't read their expressions, but close enough to see the tan of their faces aimed at the sky. They turned away and scurried in different directions, diving for shelter. In seconds, the streets were empty and the sky was black.

Though Tal knew this was only a vision of the past, his heart raced as if it were happening to him now. The wind ripped and the sea swelled, filled with white-caps. He dared to tip his head up to see what was above him.

It appeared to be black, billowing smoke, but it took the form of a hand. A hand that stretched across the sky, its finger-tips reaching toward the horizon, the heel of its palm sagging over the wildflower fields behind Beezus. It was the Hand of Calamity.

Tal's breath lodged in his throat. He fought the urge to shut his eyes and spare himself witnessing the destruction of Beezus, but his request to see Naomi's birth story didn't line up with this vision. This couldn't be when Calamity destroyed Beezus when Namoi was a child, because Naomi was six years old when her home was destroyed. This had to be something else. Something from the past that he was entirely unaware of.

Then a burst of light ripped the sky apart and a shining hand with long, golden fingers that almost took up the whole sky appeared. This, Tal knew, was The Hand of Protection. Protection reached for The Hand of Calamity and gripped its wrist, as if holding it prisoner. It was then that Tal noticed a darker black spot on Calamity's palm, like the palm had been cut open. The darker spot dripped like blood, and Tal realized that it was, in fact, blood. Calamity's blood was black, only a deeper shade than the color of the hand itself. It was a black that the King had never seen in his lifetime.

Calamity writhed in Protection's grip, fighting to escape, but Protection held on with a ferociousness. It tipped Calamity's palm toward Beezus and gave a shake. A single drop of black blood fell from Calamity's sliced-open palm. The drop fell down to the shore, landing on the pebbly beach like a splash of paint, but it soaked into the ground, disappearing and leaving no stain.

A whirlwind of air spun above Tal's head as the two hands twisted with one another in a tornado of black and gold. A low, swooshing sound roared across the sky and the two hands sucked down to a single dot, then disappeared.

The blue skies blinked back into place and the sun beat down on the white-domed village again. It was as if the supreme beings had never been there.

Except for a single spot on Beezus's shoreline.

The pebbles that littered the sand parted, creating a circle around the spot where Calamity's black blood had dropped. The sand swirled and shifted as something rose from beneath the ground. Tal watched with blinking eyes as a small, wailing body emerged from the sand.

An infant.

Its skin was red, its fuzzy hair still wet, and it screamed. Helpless, frightened.

"A child!" Tal shouted, no longer remembering he was merely watching events of the past. "Somebody get the child!"

But the infant continued to wail.

"Please spare the child!" Tal screamed louder. "Somebody—"

Then a woman was sprinting across the shore toward the baby. Her dress clung to her legs as she ran, and she held her hair in place with a hand.

"Pieter!" the woman cried. "Pieter, come quick!"

Another person—a young man—emerged from a cottage closest to the shore. He had dark hair and dark skin, just like everyone else in Beezus. He was agile, arriving at the woman in seconds. By now the woman had picked up the infant and held it close to her chest, shushing it and rocking it as she sat on her knees.

"Sandra, was the infant left here when everyone fled?" Pieter asked.

Sandra shook her head, tears filling her eyes. "He was dropped here. I saw it happen when I peeked out the window. I—"

"Drop the infant!" Pieter exclaimed. "It's a product of the Outer Void!"

"No!" Sandra sobbed, holding the child closer to her chest. "He's too young! He'll die!"

"Listen." Pieter grabbed Sandra's head and held it against his own chest. "You don't know what you're saying. This child is not of our world. Haven't you seen what has already happened to Thãen? Witches and Magnificents? Supreme beings clouding our skies? This child is likely just as dangerous."

Sandra pulled away and locked eyes with Pieter, tears covering her cheeks. "Or this child may be able to help us."

Pieter froze, his knees digging into the sand, his hands on his wife's shoulders. "If we take the child in, there will be questions from others. We would be risking everything."

"But think of the alternative," she begged. "We leave him to die?" She sat up and leaned into his face. "I know you, Pieter Massoud. You wouldn't let an innocent child die."

Tal flinched, his eyes darting from Pieter to Sandra, then to the infant. The infant wasn't Naomi Massoud, but the first of her bloodline. And Pieter Massoud was merely the man who would decide to take the child in, giving him his own last name.

It wasn't the name Massoud that gave this bloodline power, it was the origin story that did. The moment a drop of blood fell from Calamity's palm and birthed an infant in the sand, an infant that would eventually grow to lead a normal life and procreate, furthering the human name Massoud, but passing on its godlike blood. This infant wasn't fully human. It had been created by Calamity. And now Tal knew that Calamity's blood ran in Naomi Massoud's veins.

Tal whipped his head out of the basin and gasped. He was back in the four-walled space behind his throne. The liquid in the basin sat still, as if it hadn't just been disturbed. But Tal's hands shook as he wiped his eyes. He had seen what he had asked to see, and it wasn't what he expected. Massouds were supposed to have power over Calamity, not be a part of it.

He dropped to his knees and took mouthfuls of air. The thoughts in his head spiraled so fast he thought he might vomit. But he shut his eyes and breathed. Slowly. He tried to sort it out. His first thought was that maybe he actually should kill Naomi Massoud, but then he remembered that Calamity wanted her dead. Why would Calamity want to kill something that is a part of itself? The only logical answer was that Naomi truly did have power over The Dark Hand. And if she had power over The Dark Hand, then she was the only weapon that could truly save Thãen from Calamity.

But Tal had to keep Calamity on his side if he wanted to

help Naomi somehow. He had to play the game with the evil god.

"I'll kill Naomi Massoud," he whispered into the air so Calamity could hear.

But he knew in his heart that he wouldn't. He just had to lie long enough.

CHAPTER THIRTEEN

Naomi's bones throbbed from the cold as she rode on Ferrin's horse. For the last two days the rain hadn't let up. Now, as the peaks of Le'Gar finally pierced through the trees ahead, the rain seemed to fall even harder. It pounded against Naomi's back, and because nature had spoken to her before, she imagined that perhaps the rain was a sort of warning. A foreboding one. One that told her to tread carefully. But she knew Le'Gar needed her.

Ferrin was on foot, leading his horse and Naomi forward by the reins. The horses were exhausted from fighting the mud. The worst part about the whole scenario was that they were going to have to leave the horses somewhere before entering Le'Gar. There was no way for them to sneak into the city with three horses in tow. But when Vira suggested ditching the horses, Ferrin had snapped at her, clearly not wanting to betray his steed. Ferrin had been quiet since, not mentioning the inevitable. Until now. Because the stone bridge that stretched over a narrow stream and led into Le'Gar lay ahead. It was barely visible between the night sky and the black clouds, but the lanterns caged into Le'Gar's outer wall sat aflame, flickering in the wind, illuminating the three guards standing at the end of the bridge, facing the mountains.

"Dismount," Ferrin whispered, reaching up to help Naomi down.

She grabbed his hand and landed in a slick of mud. Vira and Millicent dropped down next to Hux. Poor Millicent looked like a drowned rat, even though Vira did her best to shield her daughter from the rain. The girl shivered, her teeth audibly chattering.

Naomi glanced at her, an ache throbbing into her chest at what the young girl was having to endure, but the sound of another set of chattering teeth drew her attention away from Millie and to Ferrin instead. His teeth were chattering, too. And his hands shook as he pulled the bit and bridle off his horse's muzzle.

Naomi kept her voice low as she turned to him. "Are you okay?"

He tucked the horse's headgear under his arm and kept his head bent. "I'm cold." He leaned forward and rested his head on his horse's neck. For a long moment he stayed that way, eyes closed, not saying a word. Then he gave the horse a solid pat and mumbled, "You can go wherever you wish, but you can always come back."

Naomi watched as the horse pranced sideways, seeming confused as to why it was no longer following Ferrin's lead.

"It's okay," Ferrin urged his horse onward, "you're free to go. For now, at least."

Hux's horse dashed into the mountains without hesitation. Vira's horse quickly followed suit, charging up the soaking mountain.

"Go," Ferrin ordered again, nudging his horse's rear. "Please. Don't make this harder than it has to be."

The horse trotted away from them, looking over its shoulder before finally disappearing into the dark.

Naomi touched Ferrin's arm. "I'm sorry."

He shook water from his hair and stepped away from her. "It has to be this way."

She pulled her hand back into herself, feeling the distance he physically put between them. But she didn't take it personally. She knew by now that Ferrin tended to feel uncomfortable when emotion was involved. And watching his life-long, obedient horse charge into the mountains most likely tore him apart.

"Get close," Ferrin ordered, as if he didn't hurt at all. "I'll need to summon invisibility around us at least until we get deeper into Le'Gar's streets."

The group pressed together. Naomi stood between Ferrin's shoulder and Vira's back. They moved as a mass toward the stone bridge, nicking each other's heels as they went. Ferrin squeezed Naomi's shoulder and took a deep breath.

Then they arrived at the bridge.

One of the guards, a woman, nudged the other male guard in the bicep. "Hey," she mumbled and pointed into the mountain. "Did you hear that? Sounded like the hooves of horses."

The male guard attempted to get a deeper look into the trees, but everything was black and suppressed by a wall of rain. "It's raining. Everything sounds strange."

Ferrin gently guided Naomi forward, pulling the others along with her. They moved as one, right between the two guards. A gargoyle with a human body and dragon wings hung over the bridge on the ledge of Le'Gar's outer wall. When Naomi passed underneath it, she dared to glance up. It looked directly at her, its two fangs flashing in a glint of lightning.

The gargoyles never scared her before, but this one's stare

was more human than stone, and its fangs didn't show as a grin, but a sneer.

She must have stopped moving for a moment, because Ferrin nearly plowed over her. He caught himself with her shoulders and Hux braced himself as the rest of the group tipped forward, each relying on the other.

"Keep moving," Ferrin's whisper sizzled in her ear.

His tone struck her core and she regained her balance, continuing on. They crossed into the city, entirely unseen.

The cobblestone streets were just as gray and slick as Naomi remembered. When Ferrin took the lead and guided them down one of the main roads, a sense of home settled in her heart, even though this was the least welcoming situation she could have asked for. The street curved like a moving snake, passing between textured rock buildings with iron-framed windows of blown glass. The only lanterns that remained lit in the storm were the ones on black poles that were entirely enclosed by glass.

Thunder cracked in the sky and Ferrin lifted a hand. "We're no longer invisible," he said, "but stick close and follow me."

Naomi stayed at his back as he hung close to the wall of the building on her right. The shadows were darker here. But even so, when lightning flashed, the street illuminated for a split second, sending Naomi's stomach into a curl. She didn't come all this way to get caught.

She didn't come all this way to be found.

Wiping water from her lips, she swallowed her fear and focused on Ferrin's back. He seemed to know exactly where he was going, and she trusted him. But lighting flashed again, and when Naomi looked up, all the gargoyles lining the street above were looking down, watching her.

A calmness washed over her. The gargoyles knew she was

back, and that meant they would protect her while she was here. They had protected her before, she knew they would protect her again.

CHAPTER FOURTEEN

Ferrin stopped the group outside of a rotting, wooden door that sank deep into the stone of one of the buildings lining the street. The stone arch over the door was low, forcing Ferrin to duck as he leaned in to knock.

Rainwater dripped off the arch's ledge and fell down Naomi's back. She shivered and wished the rain would let up. It had been downpouring for ages now. Surely her bones were ice at this point. *Please, just fall a little easier,* she begged.

The constant *pat, pat, pat* of the raindrops on the stone gradually became more spread out. *Paaat. Paaat. Paaat.*

Naomi looked up, letting the rain splash in her eyes. The clouds were a shade lighter, the next rumble of thunder a tad farther off.

Vira looked up too, noticing the sudden change. "Naomi?"

"Yes," Naomi said slowly. "I asked for it. I don't know why I didn't ask sooner."

But had she actually thought of asking the rain to stop hours ago, she would have been too afraid to try. She didn't want to know the feeling of playing god. Controlling the skies felt daunting.

"Even the storm obeys you," Hux marveled from the back of the group.

Millicent tugged on Naomi's arm. "Can you make it stop?"

Naomi shook her head.

Then the door swung open and a wash of warm air floated out to the drenched travelers.

An old man stood in the doorway. His head of hair and his beard were gray. He wore a white buttoned shirt with a brown vest over it. He appeared strangely scholarly, and unsurprisingly familiar to Naomi. Though she hadn't seen the old man since she arrived in Le'Gar as a child, she had never forgotten his face. The face of the old man from the docks, the same one who had helped her pass off her forged legal papers. He had knocked them into the dirt, soiling them to look appropriately old when she was entering Le'Gar as Naomi Smyth, her alias. He had saved her from having her documents questioned.

For a moment there was silence. The old man stood still, gazing at Ferrin, and Ferrin stood just as stuck.

The rain fell lightly, filling in the quiet.

Then the old man's mouth parted in a joyous, relaxed smile. "Welcome home, Ferrin."

Ferrin didn't move. His shoulders sagged forward, his head slightly bent. "I've brought her," he finally said, sputtering through his chattering teeth. "Because she wanted to return."

Naomi peered over Ferrin's shoulder at the old man. "Are you Eli?"

Eli smiled. "I am."

"I thought so," Naomi said.

Ferrin had told Naomi about how Eli took him in when he was young and afraid to use his powers. Eli was a strong, wise, Magnificent, and he had been protecting Massouds for over a century. But Eli and Ferrin had tension between them now, after a Massoud that Eli was protecting died due to a mistake on Ferrin's behalf. Ferrin had admitted to Naomi more than once how much he blames and hates himself, but to Naomi, Eli didn't seem the least bit bothered to see Ferrin standing on his doorstep now. The only person who seemed bothered was Ferrin.

Well, if Ferrin wasn't going to ask, she was. "Can we come in? We're soaked."

Eli laughed lightly and stepped aside. "That's been the plan all along, my friends. Please, get out of the rain."

The group slogged in and when Eli shut the door behind them, the sound of the rain was finally muffled. The air at last dry.

Naomi glanced around the room. A fire leapt in the red-brick fireplace built into the gray stone wall. Cushioned chairs and a leather sofa sat facing the fireplace. The wall to the right was just a massive bookshelf, and an open, curved doorway at the back of the room led to another area Naomi couldn't see into.

Eli folded his hands at his stomach. "I'm glad you made it here safely. Any trouble along the way?"

Hux and Naomi shared a glance.

"We came across some Riders of Le'Gar," Hux informed. "Three of which were dead. One remains though—Saul, and he has a golden witch in tow."

"I assume you're Hux," Eli stated, offering a hand.

Hux shook it with a firm grasp. "Yes, though you've probably only heard poor things about me."

Eli motioned to Hux's right arm. "I wouldn't say poor. A Lead Rider with a disability is practically unheard of. I'd say you rose above the rest."

Hux hesitated, as if caught off guard. "I was talking about my treason."

"Ah," Eli said, tilting his head sideways. "That. Treason isn't always bad. Especially when your reasoning for committing it is based on higher morals."

Hux nodded but remained quiet.

"Don't forget what you've accomplished in your life," Eli went on, staring Hux down like a hawk. "You think you're of lesser value because you are a human in the presence of golden witches and Magnificents, but that's not true. Where would the quill be now if it weren't for you?"

Eli didn't give Hux a chance to answer before he moved on to Vira, who held Millicent by the shoulders.

"Vira," he spoke with awe. "You have been faithful to the visions you were blessed with." He touched his chest. "It is a great honor to stand in your presence. Well done." He lowered his stare to Millicent. "And who is this?"

"My daughter." Vira gripped the girl's shoulders even tighter. "I'll do anything to keep her safe. It's why she's here."

"Of course," Eli agreed. "The duty of a mother is one that many don't understand, but you seem to understand. Well done on all accounts, Vira. I look forward to pressing onward together."

Eli looked to the arched doorway that led to the next room and there stood a woman beneath it.

Naomi's heart leapt when she saw the woman. It was Deirdre. The librarian, the one who gave her a safe place to stay in Le'Gar.

Deirdre's skin looked dry and cracked, her eyes dull. But life flooded into them when she saw Naomi.

"You've made it back, Ms. Smyth," the librarian praised.

Naomi didn't have the same sing-song voice in her response. "You knew all along."

Deirdre flattened the front of her dress with her hands. "Yes, I knew. But I couldn't tell you. I understand if that makes you upset."

"I'm not upset," Naomi quickly reassured. "I'm grateful that you helped me, even though it was dangerous for you to do so."

Millicent sneezed and Deirdre wandered over to her and Vira.

"I have dry clothes," Deirdre offered. "And two rooms in the back. Shall we get your girl warm?"

Vira nodded. "I would appreciate that."

Deirdre led Millicent and Vira through the doorway and away to the second half of the home.

"Is this your home?" Naomi asked Eli.

"It is. It's humble. It's fairly hidden. And it can also hide me if need be."

"How?" Ferrin pried.

Eli wandered to the fireplace and with a wave of his hand, made the flames disappear. He pressed a brick inward and the back of the fireplace slid open, revealing a tunnel that seemed to travel into a dark abyss.

"It connects to many of the hidden passageways in the city," he revealed. "Extremely useful."

When he closed the passage off again, he waved his hand and brought the fire back. He turned to find Hux and Naomi watching him with wide eyes.

"Ah." Eli chuckled and dropped a hand onto Ferrin's shoulder. "You're used to this young Mag doing all the tricks for you, and you haven't seen him control fire, huh?"

Ferrin visibly tensed. "I can't control fire," he said numbly. "I wasn't blessed with that power."

Eli frowned at Ferrin's downcast face and removed his hand from his shoulder. He seemed to be considering whether or not to address the cold air between them, but he turned to Naomi instead.

"Do you remember me?" he finally asked.

"Of course. But back then I thought you were a mean, clumsy old man."

"And now?"

She gave a small, genuine smile. "Now I know that you were protecting me. And I don't think I can offer enough thanks."

His eyes crinkled with his reply. "I don't look for thanks. I only look for a woman who is willing and able to face The Dark Hand, and I know I've found her."

CHAPTER FIFTEEN

With only three hours left until dawn, Eli suggested everyone to rest, adding that when the sun came up, questions would be answered, and actions would be discussed.

And Naomi had a lot of questions. They clogged her brain as she lay in front of the fireplace on the knitted rug that dug into her back. She knew she wouldn't sleep, but she at least had to pretend like she was trying, because Ferrin was sprawled out on the leather couch behind her and she didn't want any reason to have to talk to him. He had been rather distant toward Eli since their arrival, and Naomi didn't think that was fair of him. Eli was still risking everything by being faithful to the call on his life. Naomi was appreciative, and Ferrin was not. That's how she saw it anyway.

She sat up and switched positions to lie on her other side, sorry she had insisted she wanted to sleep closest to the fire. The knotted rug was really beginning to annoy her. Or was it her inner agitation that was actually keeping her awake? Agitation toward Ferrin, questions about Deirdre, worries about what was next, fears about what would happen if King Tal found out she was back in Le'Gar.

"Maybe if you switch positions one more time, the rug will turn into a mattress instead," Ferrin mumbled from the couch.

Naomi sat up and faced him with a glare. He had his hands propped behind his head as he lay quite comfortably on the couch. His eyes looked just as tired as everyone else's, but apparently, he also couldn't fall asleep.

Vira had taken one of the bedrooms with Millicent, while Eli gave his own bedroom to Hux, since it sounded like Hux was growing a cough and he was running a fever. Deirdre went home for the night, and Eli took to the tunnels of Le'Gar to see if he could intercept any news entering the city regarding Saul and Estell, who were still missing. That left Ferrin and Naomi alone in the living space.

"Maybe if you and I switched places, I would be able to get comfortable," Naomi grouched.

He frowned. "You chose the floor. You wanted to be close to the fire."

"Well, I think I've changed my mind."

"Fine." He sighed and sat up. "You win."

She hugged her knees into her chest. "No, no it's fine. I was only teasing. I wouldn't make you do that."

He gave her an unsatisfied stare. "You're clearly uncomfortable down there." He stood. "Just switch with me."

She rose faster than he and strode over to the couch. "Sit." She pushed him in the chest and forced him back down.

He stared up at her and she returned the look, forcing herself not to glance away.

"You've been ungracious toward Eli," she accused. "It's bothering me."

His face fell. "Come on, Omi, not now. Okay? Please? I'm tired."

"We're all tired."

"What do you want to hear from me?" he snapped. "You know the guilt I feel coming back here. You know how embarrassed I feel to look Eli in the eyes after all these years. I made a mistake that took the life of Oliver, and Eli suffered from it, too. He loved Oliver like a son. And I loved Estell, a witch and a woman who was evil, and I couldn't see it. I was blinded." He took Naomi's hands in his. "I can't stop hating myself. And seeing Eli only reminds me of my tragic mistakes."

Naomi nodded. It wasn't the outburst she was expecting from him, but it was an invitation to have the hard conversation.

"Talk to Eli," she pleaded. "I think you're unable to forgive yourself. Do you think Eli enjoyed watching you leave?" She pulled his hands to her chest.

His expression changed as hers did. From angry to open.

"I only knew you for a short time, and leaving you in Mira Isla was awful. It was awful, Ferrin." Though she tried to keep her voice steady, she failed. "I don't know what you've done to me, but I care about you. And if I can feel that way in such a short time, how much more does Eli, who has known you much longer?"

He gripped her hands harder. "Don't say these things to me. I don't know what to make of them."

"You don't know how to accept kindness." She could have solved that for him ages ago. "You push everyone out as soon as they offer you a smile."

"That's not true."

She sat next to him, her fingers still wrapped in his. "Yes, it is. And it hurts me to watch you live that way."

"No," he begged. "Please don't blame your hurt on me."

"That's not what I'm trying to do." She let go of his hands and grabbed the sides of his face. "Look at me."

He did, though his eyes looked frightened.

"I forgive you for what happened to Oliver Massaud, my ancestor," she said firmly. "I forgive you."

A short gasp caught in his throat and he leaned forward, collapsing into her chest. She held his head in the crook of her arm and pressed her lips to the top of his head, just like she had the day she left him in Mira Isla. Only this time she didn't have to leave him, and she didn't have to pretend to feel strong.

"Stop hurting yourself," she whispered into his hair.

His fingers dug into her back as his lips moved against her chest. "I don't want to live this way anymore."

"So don't." She didn't say it in a demeaning way, but in an honest, allowing tone. He didn't need her permission to move on, but he needed her help. Even if he never admitted it. "You've been forgiven, and it's time to believe that."

He lifted his face to see hers. "How am I supposed to walk in redemption when I don't deserve it?"

"Forgiveness isn't earned, and forgiveness isn't temporary." She brushed stray hair away from his forehead. "It won't run out. Consider your mistakes forgotten."

"But I can't forget."

"Then you must remind yourself of your forgiveness every day," she instructed. "Don't let your mistakes follow you around like a shadow. Cut them off like a dead limb. Throw them in a fire."

He used his finger to draw a line along her jaw. "How are you so sure of these things?" His finger moved over the scar where Estell's knife had cut her and he paused on it. "Are you unphased by the things that have happened in your life?"

"No. I'm just very much aware that the soul is able to overcome more than we think, including our mistakes."

Now his calloused hand was on the side of her neck. She didn't move, hoping he would leave it there.

"I'd like to be able to do that," he said, watching her eyes drop to his mouth.

Naomi felt a shift in her heart. An unfamiliar, utterly horrifying shift. She knew Ferrin was special and she knew she missed him when he was gone, but that longing for him should have disappeared when they reunited. So why was there still a crack in her chest? A place that felt like it could only be filled with the Magnificent sitting in front of her.

"Let's do it then." She sat back, away from the touch of his hand, watching it fall away from her neck. "Lean into what we're capable of, I mean."

"Right," he whispered. "There is more to this than us."

Us. The word nearly killed her. The last *us* she had was with her parents. An us-ness that was through blood. She'd never had an *us* with someone of her choosing. And no one had ever chosen her. Not in this way. Whatever this was. Usually, she wouldn't be so bold, but it was nearly dawn and she hadn't slept, and asking something upfront didn't feel so terrifying. "Are we just work partners?"

He shook his head but said nothing.

She immediately regretted it. "I'm sorry. Of course we are."

He scooted toward her so that their knees touched and he held her by the shoulders. "I'm going to grow old, Omi."

"What?"

"If my purpose truly is to get you in a position to defeat Calamity, then when this is all over, I'll have completed the time that was allotted for me." Leaning into her, he rested his forehead against hers. "Whether we win or Calamity wins, age will catch up to me. It may be fast. I may not be here for long when this is all said and done."

The air in her lungs zipped in and out and she closed her eyes, taking in the weight of Ferrin's forehead against hers. "But what if it's slow?" she insisted. "What if you'll begin to age, but slowly, like the rest of us?"

His breath trailed over her nose. "What if I do?"

With a gasp, she shook her head. "Nothing. It's foolish of me to ask."

"Ask me."

She looked up, their noses brushing. "No."

When she pulled away, he reached for her, but she was already standing.

"Let's get through this," she breathed, curling her hands into fists as she stared at the fireplace. "We are here to stop Calamity from destroying the world as we know it. We don't need to be talking about anything else."

"I know," he groaned, rubbing his eyes. "I'm sorry."

"Don't be sorry." Her voice hitched as she lowered herself to the floor once again in an attempt to get at least thirty minutes of sleep. "I brought it up. And I shouldn't have." She curled up on her side, her back to Ferrin.

His words came out soft. "Do you want the couch?"

"No," she managed to say firmly. Not because she was actually comfortable on the floor, but because she was already crying. She swallowed over and over, attempting to keep the tears silent as they ran over the bridge of her nose and into her ear.

"I'm sorry," he said again gently.

She wasn't mad at him, but if she opened her mouth, a sob might come out. So she remained quiet, silently crying herself into a light sleep.

CHAPTER SIXTEEN

Though Naomi fell asleep, Ferrin did not. He watched her shoulders rise and fall in shallow swells as she lay curled up by the fire. He didn't want to hurt her. He never had. But now even more so. When he first found her outside of Le'Gar, he wanted to help her, but only because he wanted to redeem himself. Now, though? Now he wanted to protect her because he felt something. A desire for her.

"Please no," he whispered to himself.

He once told Naomi that he wished to never love again, and he meant it. In no way did he deserve love. But Naomi had spoken of forgiveness in a way he hadn't heard before. An unconditional forgiveness that didn't run out. Was it possible that his past truly didn't define him? Could he allow himself to feel something for her? If he did, would it be such a crime?

But then there was the mission. They had work to do, not a relationship to develop. And what would Eli say if Ferrin acted like his mistakes didn't have a hold on him anymore? Or was it possible that Eli had forgiven him, too?

Ferrin sat up. That was the question that kept pounding inside his head. If he knew that Eli had forgiven him for his past mistakes, the weight of his guilt may be able to rise from his chest. Moving on seemed possible if he knew Eli didn't hold a grudge.

Naomi suggested that Ferrin talk to Eli, and Ferrin's first thought was *no*. No, he wouldn't talk to Eli, because he was afraid the old man may hate him. But was Naiomi right? Was it possible that perhaps Eli knew of the same forgiveness that Naomi did?

"Alright," Ferrin whispered to himself.

He rose from the couch and buttoned the top of his shirt. Casting one last glance at Naomi, he padded to the front door and stepped out into the street. The streets and buildings were still wet, but the rain had stopped. Through the thinning clouds, Ferrin saw the morning sky beginning to wake in pale blues and a streak of orange.

"Eli," he spoke upward toward the clouds. "Where are you?"

The spring morning breeze rippled over Ferrin's nose and he breathed in, enjoying the light crispness.

Then a voice wafted into his brain.

The east side, it said. *The peak overlooking the harbor.*

Ferrin knew exactly where Eli was talking about. It was on the edge of the city's territory, where the buildings ended and the mountain curved, wrapping around toward the docks. The overlook was where Eli had taken Ferrin years ago to let him practice tossing energy without knocking down anything important, like a building or a tall pine tree.

The memory of the outlook now made Ferrin sad, as he thought back to the good times with Eli, but he pulled his hood over his head and stepped down the street. This street was narrower than most in Le'Gar, and it sat on a slant, which meant it got most of the city's runoff water. Streets like these housed residents who lived in poverty. It made sense why Eli would choose to dwell here. The Riders of Le'Gar rarely found a reason to travel through these parts.

Soon enough, Ferrin was striding across a wide, four-way intersection, hands in his pockets and head down. But a cracking sound drew his focus upward and he watched a gargoyle with curled horns spread its wings and stretch toward the rising sun. The image struck Ferrin cold, and he stopped, gazing in awe. All the years he lived in Le'Gar, the gargoyles had felt menacing to him, like they would eat him up if he gave them the chance.

They felt different to him now. Beautiful maybe. Or majestic.

He allowed himself another moment to gaze before continuing down a long street lined with black lamp posts, still lit with flames.

A young boy dressed in all black appeared from a crack between buildings. He climbed up one of the lamp posts with ease and smothered the flame with a metal, bell-shaped device. Ferrin watched as the boy dropped back to the ground and moved on to the next pole, after giving Ferrin a slight wave.

Ferrin waved back and continued to stroll. The boy must be a lantern snuffer, the job that Naomi used to have. A humble job. A job for a nobody. But Ferrin knew that Naomi wasn't a nobody. Even if she had nothing to do with bringing down Calamity, she was *somebody* to him.

A stone bridge aged with moss crossed a stream that rushed downward toward the Desarian sea, and Ferrin crossed over it. The towering pines ahead were dark brown from being wet, and their branches dripped with leftover raindrops, and for a moment, away from everything, all felt right with the world.

He sprinted into the trees and inhaled deeply.

But his feet slowed and his arms fell back at his sides as he approached the outlook point. The tall pines thinned out and rocky ground took over, jutting out over the mist that lay over the city to the left and the docks below.

Eli stood on the edge of the overlook with his back to Ferrin. But Ferrin knew Eli felt him approach. The old man always did.

Now Ferrin stood behind him, only a few feet away.

"Can't sleep?" Eli asked, as if he were questioning the sky in front of him.

Ferrin shoved his hands into his pockets. "A leather couch isn't the most comfortable arrangement."

Eli turned sideways, giving Ferrin a scheming eye. "You still prefer to dwell in the mountains?"

"No." Ferrin looked down at his own feet. "I don't think so."

Eli's face softened as he took a step toward him. "Then why didn't you return home sooner?"

Ferrin lifted his eyes, and for the first time since he'd arrived back to this soggy city, he fully took in Eli before him. The old man's face hadn't aged much. His eyebrows were still just as gray as his beard, and his posture was still semi-hunched under his cloak. But the crinkles at the corners of his eyes were shallow, as if he hadn't smiled in years.

"You must have wanted to kill me yourself," Ferrin finally said. "For betraying you the way I did."

Eli shut his eyes. "Fin. Do you not remember the day you left?"

"I remember it well enough," he groveled. "You didn't want me to go, but I knew that eventually you'd kill me in my sleep if I stayed."

"In what world would I do that?" Eli asked, his voice as calm as a dead wind.

"Don't lie," Ferrin said, voice rising. "I killed Oliver."

"You didn't kill anyone," Eli bellowed back. "Listen to me." He stepped forward and Ferrin stepped back. "No, young Mag, come here." Eli grabbed the back of Ferrin's head and pulled him close to face him. "Look at me."

Ferrin looked up, a glare glazing over his moist eyes. "I can't look at you," he admitted through a wobbly breath. "I only see my mistakes."

"Because you're blinded by them." Eli was stern, but gentle. "You didn't kill Oliver. Estell did. And you aren't responsible for her actions. You are only responsible for yourself."

"How can I make it right? Between you and me?"

Eli tapped his own heart with his free hand. "There is nothing bitter in here toward you. I never wanted you to leave, my friend. Watching you leave was the worst hurt of all."

Ferrin ground his teeth together and exhaled. "You forgive me?"

"There is nothing to forgive." He grabbed Ferrin's shoulders. "Let it go. You're the only one who hasn't forgiven you, and that will kill you if you keep going this way."

Ferrin held a hand over his face. "It's already destroyed me."

"That's the most precious thing about the soul," Eli soothed. "It can rise again from the grave."

CHAPTER SEVENTEEN

Ferrin and Eli strode side by side back into the city. Golden rays of sun hit the tips of the gargoyles and glinted off the bells atop the King's cathedral in the distance. The two men made sure to keep their heads low and stuck to the shadowed parts of the streets.

"I do have to ask you something," Ferrin spoke carefully, keeping his voice low. "What does Deirdre have to do with all of this? Is she a golden witch?"

Eli eyed Ferrin. "No."

Ferrin tried to read his stare. "What then?"

"She has a lot of answers, Ferrin. Not all, but a lot. Some information she has, even I was unaware of."

"Like what? Does she know what we must do next?"

"She doesn't know the ending," Eli revealed. "Not all of it, anyway. But she does know the beginning."

Ferrin arched an eyebrow. "The beginning of what? Of the Massoud bloodline?"

Eli stopped and gently shoved Ferrin into the shadows behind a stone column at the edge of a wide fountain. "Deirdre was there the moment that the supreme beings collided with

Thãen," he whispered. "Protection chose her to remain here with Thãen's people until the plan to defeat Calamity was complete."

"She out-ages us," Ferrin breathed in disbelief. "Is she human?"

"She was. Now she's like the gargoyles."

"Meaning?

Eli smiled with one side of his face. "She can become like them. Stone. Unaging. Able to weather any storm."

"So why doesn't she have the power to defeat Calamity?"

"That's what's so difficult to piece together," Eli admitted. "Why Naomi? What about her bloodline gives her an advantage over people like Deirdre? Even over people like you and me? We can wield energy."

"She can control nature." Ferrin didn't mean to sound defensive, but it came out faster than he could tame it.

Eli raised his hands, fending off Ferrin's ill look. "I'm not doubting her. Graves knows I've spent my entire life dedicated to her bloodline because I've known of the power they have." He paused to search Ferrin's steel expression. "Oliver managed to uproot trees and grow wildflowers. He could tell the birds where to fly and coax fish into the harbor." He gripped Ferrin's shoulder and leaned in. "What has Naomi managed to do?"

Ferrin relaxed under the familiar touch of Eli's hand. "She created a mountain from nothing. The trees and grass speak to her. She had the ground swallow up Estell and I'm told she commanded the sea to flood a seaside farm."

Eli's lips parted and he stepped back. "Commanded the sea? She was able to command the sea?"

"Yes." Ferrin narrowed his eyes. "Is that normal for her bloodline?"

"Normal?" Eli stroked his beard. "Nothing about her bloodline is normal. But I will tell you this: Oliver never even came close to commanding the waves."

The two stood staring at each other, still hidden behind the towering column, but morning had come, and soon the streets would be full.

Eli dropped his chin along with his voice. "Let me ask you."

Ferrin nodded.

"Have you ever seen Naomi bleed?"

Ferrin skewed his lips. "What?"

"Was she ever cut? Or scraped? Have you ever seen blood come out of her skin?"

"I've seen her bleed," he confirmed, squinting. "Her jaw got sliced in Mira Isla, but it was dark outside and I was holding Vira, trying to keep her alive. I didn't pay close attention to it." He darted his eyes around the street, feeling the presence of others. "Why are you asking me about her blood? What does it mean?"

Eli pressed his lips together. "I don't know yet, but Deirdre claims that Naomi once bled black blood."

Ferrin's veins ran cold. "What would that mean?"

Eli gave a baffled shrug. "I don't know yet."

Ferrin gazed at the ground and bit his tongue. He didn't want to give Eli a reason to think Naomi was anything other than good, but Eli was on his side. "Naomi has had an encounter with Calamity." His voice flattened. "It was in Mira Isla. The Dark Hand transformed into some form of a shadowed man and approached Naomi to tell her that she was a part of itself."

"A part of Calamity? How so?"

"We don't know." Ferrin shook his head and gazed over Eli's shoulder. "But I don't want you to bring it up to her. She was terrified when Calamity said that to her. We don't know that it's true, either."

"But if she bleeds black," Eli countered, "there could be truth to—"

"I don't care," Ferrin snapped. "She's a person before she's a weapon, and if the thought of being a part of Calamity terrifies her, I won't let it be brought up. Not now." He inhaled, regulating himself. "I'm sorry, Eli, but I care about her. And she wants this to end just as much as we do."

"I'm not suggesting she's against us," Eli clarified. "I'm only pointing out that there may be more to her than we know, and it's up to us to uncover it. If we leave it buried, we may not win."

CHAPTER EIGHTEEN

When Ferrin and Eli returned home, Naomi rose from the leather couch.

"Is everything alright?" she asked through a worried breath.

"All is well," Ferrin affirmed, showing amusement through a smile. "I just went out to meet Eli when I couldn't sleep." He averted his eyes and stepped past her to the back of the home where Millicent stood beside Vira. "Rested up, Mill?"

She blushed at his nickname and nodded.

He gave her hair a slight ruffle before peering at Hux in the corner. "How's the cough?"

Hux shrugged. "Deirdre gave me a shot of whiskey, so I think I'll be fine."

"Whiskey at dawn?" Naomi teased. "I suppose that's how the outlaws do it."

Deirdre emerged from the kitchen around the corner with two cups of hot tea and shoved them into Eli's and Ferrin's hands. "Down it," she ordered, brushing back her sandy-colored hair. "It's echinacea and ginger. If a sickness plagues any of you before this is over, I will be more than angry. I'll probably be feral and irrational."

Ferrin laughed into his mug.

"It's just a cough," Hux complained, raising his hands. "From being in the rain for days."

Deirdre eyed him, hands on her hips. "I don't care. I've been living for centuries waiting for this moment. I'm not risking anything."

Hux rolled his eyes, but stifled a cough with a grunt.

Eli cleared his throat. "I'd like to take this time to share information. Deirdre and I have a lot to share, and I'm sure you all do as well." He waved toward the fireplace that was no longer lit. "Why don't we sit over here, and I'll get the fire going again."

The crew shuffled toward the fireplace. Ferrin sat on the ground, propping an arm over his knee. He reached into his pocket and drew out two dice, and handed them to Millicent, who had sat right next to him.

"This conversation might be boring," he whispered to her. "Do you know any dice games?"

She nodded in excitement and turned away from him to begin her play.

Vira smiled at Ferrin in thanks as she sat on the leather couch between Naomi and Deirdre.

Naomi felt her stomach clench at Ferrin's kindness toward Millicent. When he looked her way, she made sure to turn her eyes to Eli, who had taken a seat in one of the cushioned chairs facing the fire, Hux occupying the other.

Eli leaned forward and rested his elbows on his knees. "Let's lay it all out in the open."

"What are the risks we face?" Vira asked. "If we lay it all out, what could happen? We have every reason to trust you, Eli, but no experience to back up our reasoning."

"I've had experience," Ferrin defended from the floor. "I vouch for him. He's been in the fight longer than all of us. Except for Deirdre—she's outlived us all."

All eyes turned to Deirdre. The mysterious woman who seemed to be a sort of sidekick to Eli.

Deirdre sat forward. "It's true. I've been here longer than the rest of you, and I promise when this conversation is over you will know everything I do." She smiled at Naomi sitting next to her. "I'm sorry I could never tell you. The best I could do was give you a place to stay."

Naomi laid a hand on Deirdre's arm. "You don't have to apologize. I understand the weight you must carry."

"How old *are* you?" Hux inquired.

"I'm centuries old. Over 2,000 years."

Ferrin choked on his tea. "You're *what*?"

Millicent looked up from her dice. "I thought Magnificents were only men."

"I'm not a Magnificent," Deirdre softly corrected.

Vira narrowed her eyes. "Golden witches aren't semi-mortal."

Deirdre lifted a finger. "Neither am I a golden witch." She rolled her shoulders back and her arms rippled with feathers before her entire being morphed to stone. Her eyes thudded into a solid tone and her facial features flattened into the rough roundness of a stone angel. She sat still, frozen to the couch.

Naomi leaned into Vira, her heart racing.

Millicent hid behind Ferrin.

The sound of grinding and clicking rock echoed in the room as Deirdre maneuvered herself back into her human form. Once again, she sat on the leather couch as if no different than the others in the room.

"What in the grave was that?" Ferrin roared.

"Mavelic made me into a stone gargoyle," Deirdre explained, attempting to pacify the shocked faces in the room.

Naomi thought for a moment before she said, "Who is Mavelic?"

"The supreme beings have names," Deirdre revealed. She held one palm up. "We have The Hand of Protection, who is Mavelic." She held up her other hand. "And we have The Hand of Calamity. Hilith. And their names hold power. Saying their names out loud may stir them up in a way we aren't prepared for, but for the sake of revealing everything I know, I will tell you their names this once."

Ferrin cleared his throat. "Eli said you were alive when Protection found Thãen."

She nodded. "I was. I was sixteen and living here in Le'Gar, though the buildings were far fewer and there were no gargoyles."

Naomi imagined Le'Gar without its magnificent beasts and decided she wouldn't have liked it that way. They were often spooky, yes, but they were also what made her city what it was.

"What happened when Protection found Thãen?" Naomi asked.

Deirdre smiled, a small, remembering kind of smile. "Our world was entirely human. There were no Magnificents, no golden witches, and no magic. We had a summer of constant rain. I remember because everyone was sad. Joy was hard to muster up in the days of endless storms. But one day an odd, extremely bright sun rose in the sky, chasing away the storm in the middle of the day. Only it wasn't the normal sun. It was too golden, too fierce. The Hand of Protection had found us.

"Up there in the Outer Void, Protection had found our world and decided to hold onto us. It gave us days of sun, flourishing crops, vibrant flowers, gentle nights. I felt as though a savior had seen our world and knew we were the ones who needed saving."

"Wow," Naomi breathed. "That sounds like paradise."

"It felt like it," Deirdre whispered, as she stared into the fireplace's flames. "I would tend the gardens on my parents' farm and thank Protection over and over for choosing us, and I felt that Protection spoke back. I would get this feeling. This affirming warmth that the thoughts I had and the prayers I prayed were heard.

"But then the magic started to show up. At first it was seen in nature—in deer that would prance through the trees and disappear in plain sight, or in rivers that sometimes whispered audible words. Then magic bestowed upon people. Some humans were able to accomplish impossible actions, like moving energy as if it were a physically tangible object."

"Like Magnificents," Ferrin deduced.

"Like Magnificents," Deirdre echoed. "Protection found us, a world full of humans, and birthed Magnificents and golden witches out of us."

"But why?" Naomi asked. "It's a little invasive if you ask me. And frightening."

"We were all frightened, yes," Deirdre agreed. "But we didn't know that Protection was giving us weapons for our own good."

Vira nodded affirmingly, seeming to get the picture. "Protection knew Calamity was out there. Mavelic knew Hilith was nearing Thãen, didn't it?"

Deirdre pointed an approving finger at Vira. "Exactly. Protection found us, humans, completely naked and vulnerable to the Outer Void. It knew that when Calamity stumbled upon us, too, we wouldn't have a fighting chance against it."

Hux crossed his arms. "So Protection armed Thãen by giving us Magnificents and golden witches? That's believable and understandable, but isn't it Protection's job to, uh, protect us? Hence the name. Why do we have to protect ourselves?"

Deirdre faced him. "Protection holds us, Hux, but that doesn't mean Protection has power that Calamity doesn't. They may have equal strength, or one may have more than the other. We don't know. What we do know is that humans didn't stand a chance against the supreme beings, so Protection gave us that chance."

"Did it work?" Millicent piped up.

All eyes turned to her, as she peered up from Ferrin's side.

"Did what work, love?" Vira questioned.

"Did Calamity try to take Thãen but failed? Is that why Calamity is so angry with us?"

Vira nodded. "Calamity hasn't been able to claim us. The fight is still happening. No one has won. No one has lost."

Ferrin stared down at the little girl whose face was clouded with fear. "But that's why we're here," he reassured. "You don't have to be afraid. We are figuring out how to end this war."

Deirdre took Naomi's hands in hers. "Look at me."

Naomi did, eyes wide.

"Your bloodline was created at the same time Magnificents and golden witches were created," Deirdre explained. "I know because Protection told me."

Naomi squeezed Deirdre's hands. "Really? Protection spoke to you?"

"Protection appeared to me in a dream," she said, just above a whisper. "It was in the form of a man made of light and fire. I knew, even though I was dreaming, that it was Protection. I remember word for word what it said to me: *Deirdre Lloyd, look to the skies and see your new companions. Spellbind them to protect this city until the one from the bloodline Massoud comes with a quill to set them free. Then my plan to keep your world safe will come to pass, and Calamity will be blotted out.*"

Naomi touched her chest, feeling the words as a weight on her soul. To know that Protection had spoken her last name with such promise, as if she really did have something to give in all this.

"When I woke up," Deirdre went on, "I ran outside and looked to the sky, just like Protection said I should, and that's when I saw the gargoyles. They appeared overnight, as if dropped from the sky, which I suppose they were. So I spoke words that came to me without thought: *In the name of Mavelic, I spellbind you to your positions to watch over Le'Gar, protect its people, and above all, shield every Massoud that may walk these stone streets. May you never leave your posts, and may your mouths be sealed from speaking knowledge to any human, golden witch, or Magnificent.*"

Ferrin ran a hand over his hair. "Wow." He exhaled and looked up. "It was you. We were always told a golden witch cast the enchantment spell on the gargoyles."

Deirdre shrugged. "Truth gets lost through centuries, but it doesn't matter that I was the one to enchant them. What matters is that Naomi will release them. The Massoud who holds the quill can set the plan in motion, but I don't know how to set the plan in motion. Protection never gave me that knowledge."

"But why did Protection have to make a plan in the first place?" said Hux. "You said the plan will be set in motion and Calamity will be blotted out, so this plan you're speaking about is what will help us destroy The Dark Hand, right?"

"Yes," Deirdre affirmed. "Protection knew that Calamity would put up a fight to hold Thãen for itself, so it set up an intricate plan to enable the people of our world to win."

Millicent had lost interest in her dice game. "Why does Calamity want to hold us?"

"Calamity wants to be the most powerful god in the Outer

Void," Deirdre said, cold. "The Dark Hand is like a king who can never have enough riches, power, and influence. Holding a world would give a god much power and reverence."

"Why wouldn't Protection just destroy Calamity itself?" Naomi wondered. "It seems awfully ridiculous for Protection to leave us to protect ourselves with a hidden plan. We aren't the supreme beings."

Deirdre pointed at her. "But *you* are."

Naomi shook her head. "I have powers that can control nature and nature speaks to me, but I'm not a god."

"You are," Ferrin said quietly.

Naomi turned to look at him. "And how would you know that?"

"Braham told me. And I believe him."

"I'm not a god," Naomi said again.

Deirdre put her palms on Naomi's shoulders. "Something about you gives you power over Calamity. Power that Protection doesn't have. Naomi, do you understand what I'm saying? Protection put an intricate plan in place centuries ago that is now unfolding. It knew that one day we would come to this moment in time when our world is tipping and Calamity is gaining the upper hand."

"But I can't do anything about it," Naomi uttered, panicked breaths taking up her throat. "I don't know the plan." Irritation took over. "What's the use of the plan if it's hidden? Why would Protection leave us without answers that we need?"

"We have the answers," Deirdre argued. "You have the key, yes?"

"The quill?"

"Yes, the quill. And you have the ink for the quill."

Naomi shrugged her shoulders out of Deirdre's grasp. "Yes, yes, I have all of that, but what am I supposed to do with it? We have the pieces, not the answers. I'm not the answer. If I don't even know who I am, how am I supposed to do this?" She stood, heat rising along her neck.

Ferrin stood, too, facing Deidre. "Alright, quit putting all the pressure on her."

"I'm not trying to," Deirdre defended with raised hands. "You wanted answers, and these are the answers."

Flabbergasted, Ferrin waved a hand toward Naomi. "She's overwhelmed!"

"Ferrin," Naomi tried.

"You're forcing her to give answers," he kept going. "It's unfair and it's confusing."

"Ferrin," Naomi said again, more stern this time. "It's alright."

He lowered his hand and stared at her, shaking his head. "You don't have to prove anything."

"I'm not trying to prove anything," she reassured in an attempt to settle him. "I'm nervous that I won't be strong enough to save Thãen. I'm afraid that I'm just like the other Massouds before me, that I will be the one who will fail." Her voice lingered off into a whisper.

Ferrin stepped toward her. "You?" He wrapped his hands around the sides of her head and held her face close to his. "No. You will not fail, because I won't let you. When you feel like giving up, I'll carry you. When you're afraid of death, I will go before you. When you try to carry all the weight alone, I will strip it from your back." His voice was shaking, same as his hands. "And I'd do that for you even if you weren't a Massoud. You aren't just a name, Omi."

Naomi fought off tears and gazed into his penetrating stare.

"We're partners," he said firmly, clearly convinced she was the answer to stopping the war. "*Partners.* The task isn't on you, it's on all of us." He let go of her head and stepped back. "Look around." He waved an arm over the group. "See us before you.

Vira has been trying to find you for years. Visions given to her from Protection led her to you. And Eli has been protecting you since you crossed the Dessarian Sea. Same as Deirdre. And Hux? He found the key that you needed. Without any of them, we wouldn't be here."

For the first time, Eli spoke up. "It's a mission meant to be carried out by all—an incredibly delicate plan that must be done perfectly in order to work."

Naomi swallowed and stepped back from Ferrin to calm her heart rate. "Why is the plan hidden?"

"Because we have one chance to join the key with the lock," Deirdre revealed. "Once the plan starts, there is no turning back." She turned to Naomi. "You have the quill, which is the key, and the quill needs to write something only it knows. We need to find what the quill wants to write on to find the answer. The lock, I suppose, is the last part that needs to be revealed. We need to find the lock for your key."

"Once the key and the lock are joined, then so begins the process to eliminate Calamity." Vira stated.

Deirdre nodded, a grinding stone sound accompanying her movement. "Yes. But we must know the entire plan before we join the key with the lock...otherwise we may waste the only chance we have to destroy Calamity."

In the silence of the room, the only sound was the fire popping. Even Millicent stopped tossing the dice to the floor and looked up.

Naomi broke the silence. "So, what are we missing?"

"A person," Eli answered. "Think about it. We've all had a part to play so far, but information is still missing. There must be someone else who knows something."

Everyone cut their eyes around the room as if questioning one another. Perhaps one of them was holding onto a piece of vital information.

"Does the phrase *let it flow* mean anything to you?" Naomi asked Eli.

He raised a bushy eyebrow before shaking his head. "No. Where is the phrase from?"

"Nature has spoken it to me," she disclosed. "And I don't know what it means."

"But there may be someone who does," Eli offered. "For now, we will add that to our growing list of puzzle pieces."

"What do we do next?" Naomi pushed. "There has to be something we can do with the information we do have. We have enchanted ink and a quill that doesn't write on anything. If those two items are part of the key, then we need to find what it needs to write on."

"Yes, that must be it," Deirdre encouraged with a firm nod.

Naomi said, "Here. The lock has to be here. Nature told me to return to Le'Gar."

Eli stood, intense angles lining his face. "Then we search the city."

"The entire city?" Ferrin doubted.

"Yes. All of Le'Gar. We better split up," Eli stated. "We'll go in pairs and we'll take shifts. Deirdre will stay back with Millicent the first go-round. Vira and Hux, you'll go together, and Ferrin and Naomi will be the other pair. I'll search the inner walls and tunnels. I know those areas best."

"Then it's decided," Naomi sealed the deal. "When does the search start?"

Eli draped his cloak over his shoulders and pulled his hood up. "Now."

CHAPTER NINETEEN

Ever since Maya, Lead Rider of the King's Guard, returned to her home territory of Raina, King Leeland had gone into a bout of depression. King Leeland had sent Maya out to find Hux and arrest him. Hux had once been King Leeland's Lead Rider, but when Hux found the sacred golden quill that King Leeland wanted, Hux abandoned King Leeland and fled with the quill.

When Maya returned and told Leeland that Hux was lost and most likely dead, he had driven his fist into the bricked wall of the war room. The blood from his knuckles was still there. No one dared to touch or clean anything he didn't ask to be touched or cleaned.

Of course, Leeland wasn't angry at Maya, because he believed she was telling the truth. Especially since she returned home with only five Riders left. In fact, it was no surprise to Maya that the King took her mental health into consideration in the midst of the mess. He ordered her to have two weeks relief from duty while he sorted out the next steps.

King Leeland was greedy, but he wasn't heartless.

The relief from duty was, in fact, what Maya knew she

needed. She felt that her lie that Hux was dead might eat her alive from the inside out. But the lie was told, and what had been done was done. She'd dug the hole she was in and she had to stick with it, because whenever she had doubts, she would think about Hux's face when she attempted to arrest him, as he cried over a dying golden witch in Mira Isla.

"You don't know the weight!" he had shouted.

The image paralyzed Maya. But she did not understand him. He had acted like committing treason and running off with the quill meant more to him than simply keeping the quill for himself, for power. If not for power, why else would Hux keep the quill?

Now, for the fourth day in a row, Maya left the hub of the city of Raina and wandered into the woods that descended down the mountainside. Spring had exploded, and the trees were flushed with brand-new green. The rivers flowing through Raina's city ran down the mountain here, webbing out into multiple streams. The streams were tinted red, but not as red as the rivers in the city. As the water flowed away from the city, it gradually faded to a faint, pink-ish hue, until eventually, farther down the mountain, the water was fully clear.

Maya never gave the rivers much thought—they were always red, and that was normal to her. But now that she walked along one of the many streams, she had to wonder. Were the stories true? Were the rivers actually red because ink fell with the rain over Raina? If that were so, would that mean the Outer Void had something to do with it? She wasn't sure how the Outer Void worked or how it was even positioned in relation to Thãen. In her imagination, the Outer Void laid behind the sky. Where else would it be? And rain fell from up there. So it was possible that red ink did indeed fall from the Outer Void.

She shoved her dreadlocks behind her shoulders and

squatted down at the creek's edge. The pink water gurgled in a peaceful song. But her heart was far from peaceful. Ever since Thãen tipped, her thoughts had derailed. Here she was, holding the position of Lead Rider, the position she had longed for since childhood, but only because Hux had given it up. No. He had thrown it away. He chose treason over duty, and for the last month, she had started to understand why.

The Hand of Calamity, the Dark Hand, was closing in, and Hux had found himself with a girl who could stop it.

Maya dipped her fingers in the water and let the chill sting her skin. Nothing was right in the world. Nothing was in order in her kingdom. She was a liar, and her king was power hungry.

What would it be like, she thought, *if Hux is right and there is an end to the oppression of Calamity?*

For a moment her heart soared at the thought of total freedom. But then something at the bottom of the creek caught her eye.

She leaned forward and shoved her hand deeper into the water. Soggy, deteriorating leaves caked the creek floor, but a round piece of metal poked out of the mud beneath them. She swept the slimy leaves aside and wrapped her palm around the piece. It was smaller than her palm but embedded deeply in the creek bed, as if the wide metal rod had been buried. No amount of tugging would release it, and though she would have tried longer, the unexpected sound of trumpets calling for all to come together rang out from Raina's castle.

Maya stumbled backward as she pulled her hand from the water. The trumpets were only used by Calvary if there was an emergency. A turn of events. Something deeply important.

Pushing herself up, Maya set off in a sprint back toward the city, but she staggered when her foot caved into the ground. She fell to one knee and lifted her foot out of a hole. A rabbit hole was her first guess, but her hands were pressed against the ground and her face close to the dirt. Being at this level, Maya could see something she hadn't seen before.

Between the roots and moss that clung to the rocks in the soil, she could see *into* the ground. Not just into a hole, which would make sense, but gaps in the ground seemed to suggest there was a space beneath the ground here. A pit. An underground cave. A tunnel.

She swung around and peered into the hole her foot had fallen into. Here it was, clear as day, a hole in the ground that had caved because there was an open space beneath it. And though it was dark down there, Maya could see that a tunnel traveled both left and right.

A tunnel that seemed to run parallel with the creek.

The trumpets sounded in the distance again and Maya stood. She kicked fallen leaves and twigs over the hole before taking off again toward the city.

Soon she would learn what made King Leeland call for the warning trumpets, but as she ran, she vowed that he would *not* know of the tunnel she just found. Like Hux, she felt a weight. The weight of a plan unfolding. And suddenly she had adopted the same mind as he had, the mind of a treasonist. But in her heart, there was an odd sense of rightness.

You don't know the weight! Hux had accused her.

Now she wanted to scream back at him. *I do know. I'm starting to understand.*

CHAPTER TWENTY

Naomi and Ferrin melded into the busy streets of Le'Gar. The sun sat high, no clouds covered the blue sky. The smell of something roasting wafted down the street, as smoke from a fire pit outside of a meat market rose into the air. Naomi's stomach growled as they passed. Even the gargoyle with a bald head and long fingernails that was perched on the windowsill of the meat market looked hungry, his mouth drawn down as if longing to try what was cooking.

Naomi turned to Ferrin and nodded at the man standing over the fire. "Do you think I'd be recognized if I bought a piece of whatever he's cooking?"

"Did you eat before we left?"

"Bread and a banana."

"Yeah, that's not too filling, is it?"

"I'm not complaining," she said quickly. "I'm just hungry. For something real. Do you know how many times I've eaten oats and apples the past two months?" She held up all ten fingers. "More than this. I want a duck, Ferrin. I want a turkey. I want—"

Ferrin broke into a laugh. "Oh, hush already. You want a piece of what he's cooking?"

"No, I was just—"

But Ferrin was already sauntering over to the man cooking over the fire. Naomi hung back as he exchanged a few words with the meat marketer, tossed him a few coins, and walked away with a piece of steaming meat wrapped in brown paper.

Ferrin bumped into her, shoving her onward, and placed the hot paper in her hands. "There. You happy?"

She looked down at the moist, dry-rubbed piece of what looked like pork. Her mouth watered. "You didn't have to do that."

He reached into her hand and pulled off a piece of pork for himself. A mini smile touched the corners of his mouth. "You wanted it. Now you have it."

Naomi took a bite of the meat and looked down at her feet as they walked. Was that his version of saying he bought it because it made her happy? Had it been a gesture of some kind? Because lately he had been doing a lot of gestures. And though nothing in the world was right, Naomi found herself wanting more of his gestures. Even if tomorrow Thãen fell into Calamity's palm, there was still time today. There was time in the now. Was it a naive thought? Yes. Did it cloud her judgement? Possibly. But the idea of Ferrin had become a strong pull in Naomi's heart. And right now, she wanted to see where the pull would lead her.

"Hey," she said. "Let me show you where I used to live."

Before doubt took over, Naomi slipped her hand into Ferrin's and pulled him after her.

He staggered a little at the sudden change in direction, but he picked up his pace and followed.

Naomi felt his hand tighten around hers, and the pull in her chest grew.

"The key, Omi," he reminded. "That's why we're out here."

She turned and smiled at him. "We're attempting to search the whole city, aren't we? So we can start up there." With her free hand, she pointed up at the blinding sun where a tower struck the sky in the distance.

He squinted and glanced up. "You really did live with the gargoyles, huh?"

"Yes. And I want to show you. Come on."

They set off down the street. Naomi focused on his hand in hers and brought his attention upward as they went, pointing out certain gargoyles she liked or ones that Le'Garians were particularly afraid of. Occasionally Ferrin would make a remark about how he remembered some of the gargoyles and he would give his own input on his feelings toward them.

When they crossed through Center Square, Naomi let go of his hand and broke into a run. The square was packed with vendors and business men and women on their mid-day break. As Naomi weaved through them, no one gave her and Ferrin a second look. The two of them might as well be workers late for their shift. But Naomi knew the griffin at the top of the cathedral didn't think that, and she wanted to escape his eye. Not because she didn't trust him, but because if he spotted her, rumors about her appearance would waft through the city, and that meant King Tal may hear about her reappearance.

They exited Center Square, but Naomi kept running. It felt freeing, and they were almost to the abandoned steeple that held the inner staircase leading up to the roof. To her surprise, Ferrin kept up with her, running just as fast, and he was smiling. Maybe it was the sunshine, or maybe it was the warm breeze, but in this moment, Naomi could tell that he felt the same happiness as she. A happiness as light as air.

When Naomi came to the empty building with the steeple, she strode right up to the rotting front doors. With a glance over her shoulder, she made sure Ferrin was behind her before she slipped inside. He followed her into a building that had once been an armory. The layout was a simple square, and the only details on the walls were small vents to let in the outside air. There were no windows or furniture of any kind. But there was a door in the back of the building, and that's where Naomi headed.

Once again, she took Ferrin's hand and pulled him across the room. When they slipped through the door, a set of spiraling stairs led up and up and up. But the distance and the climb felt like nothing to Naomi, because she had done it so many times, and Ferrin still held onto her hand.

"You did this every day?" Ferrin panted.

Naomi grinned down at him. "Wait until you see what's next."

At the top of the stairs, another door sat in the wall of what was the top of the steeple. Ferrin didn't have to look outside to know they must be towering over the city at this height. And when Naomi shoved open the door, sunlight glittered the tops of Le'Gar's stone peaks, and the gargoyles sat at eye level across the expanse of the city. Just outside the door was a stone catwalk that crossed from the steeple to the roof of the library.

Naomi dragged him behind her as she began to cross the catwalk

"Graves," Ferrin cursed. "You never worried about falling?"

"Of course I thought about it, but I had no choice. If I wanted a roof over my head, this was my option."

Ferrin tightened his grip as they neared the middle of the catwalk. "Okay," he said, voice trembling. "I'm getting cold feet. I'm getting cold feet."

Naomi faced him. "Why? The walkway is four feet wide. You would have to *try* to fall from here."

He smiled, a glimmer of deviousness hiding behind his eyes.

"I'm joking." Then his voice fell. "I just wanted you to look at me."

She stood still, the wind playing with her loose hairs. "Why?"

"Do I have to tell you why?"

She shook her head. She already knew.

He nudged his chin forward. "You gonna keep walking? We are suspended over the city."

"I don't know," she played. "I might want to keep you here." But she stepped forward again, guiding them to the safety of the library's flat roof.

He stepped up behind her as she faced the window of her old home.

"Why would you want to keep me here?" he asked, playing along.

Naomi felt his overwhelming presence at her back, and she wanted to answer him, but seeing her old window, the last home she knew, it hurt. Because it was no longer her home, and suddenly reality struck her again.

"Naomi?" Ferrin touched her shoulders. "Are you okay?"

She turned and looked past him to the beast gargoyle that loomed on the ledge of the roof.

"There he is," she exclaimed. "I've missed him, you know."

Ferrin looked to the gargoyle. "Him?"

Naomi swallowed, keeping a pit of sorrow away, then strode over to her old beast. She placed a hand on his back of stone fur and touched one of his horns.

The beast let out a baritone sigh, and his head crunched toward her.

She wrapped her arm around his neck and stepped up on the ledge to stand beside him. "It's me," she said.

The beast set his eyes on her, but no expression was readable in them. As usual. Stone doesn't show emotion.

Naomi looked down at Ferrin, who was staring up at her on the ledge. She lowered her hand as an invitation. He took it and joined her. They stood staring out at the city that sat basking in the sun. Here, they were safe.

They were alone.

"Listen," Naomi started, twisting her fingers and fumbling over her words. "You said you may grow old quick, but—"

Ferrin shook his head. "No."

Naomi snapped her mouth closed and studied him. "You're shutting me out."

"What do you want me to do?" he whispered, shoulders sagging. "I never wanted this again."

Her voice wavered. "Wanted what?"

"Come on. We don't have to dance around it. There's something between us. I don't know when it started to grow, but it's there. You cannot deny it."

Naomi's cheeks flushed.

Ferrin chuckled and tucked her loose hair behind her ear. "You don't have to be embarrassed."

"I'm not embarrassed," she said with stubbornness.

"Okay," he gave in, "so you're not embarrassed, but you're..."

"I'm scared."

He rested his hand on the side of her neck. "Of?"

"You never wanted this. I never planned for this. But we're here."

"And?"

"And for graves' sake, Ferrin," she said, "if you age quickly when this is all over, it's going to hurt so bad."

He closed his eyes and bowed his head toward her. "I know."

In a swell of desperation, Naomi wrapped her arms around

his neck and pulled him into her. "Can you choose to stay?" she begged. "Please?"

His voice came out muffled against her neck. "I don't get to choose."

"No," she fought. "It's not fair."

Ferrin tightened his arms around her core and let out a defeated exhale into her skin. "I know."

Naomi brought her eyes to the sky. "Please let him stay," she whispered. "Please."

"Don't do that," he pleaded.

"I have no other choice." A solitary tear slid down her cheek. "If it's not up to us, it has to be up to someone else."

"I know, but it hurts to hear you ask it. It hurts to know that if I'm gone, you will feel my loss."

Naomi pulled back but kept her arms draped around his neck. "But here we are."

He let his forehead touch hers. "Here we are." A gentle thumb stroked her cheek. "This was your plan, wasn't it?"

She frowned. "What?"

"To bring me all the way up here so you could get me alone."

A mini grin lit up her face. "So what if it was?"

He kissed her forehead. "I knew you were mischievous, Miss Smyth."

She leaned into his chest and glowered up at him. "Don't 'Miss Smyth' me."

"What shall I call you, then?" he toyed.

Her chest was on the verge of bursting. She couldn't handle his voice just out of reach of her mouth anymore. "Just call me Omi."

Ferrin lowered his lips and said, "Fine. Omi." Then he met her mouth all the way.

The way he said her name warmed her core, but his kiss set

her on fire. No one had ever warned her that a kiss from a Magnificent held as much energy as a Magnificent could wield. By the time it was over her entire body was shaking.

Ferrin held the sides of her face. Naomi put her hands on his.

"I pray you can stay," she said, "that you will age as I do. That I won't lose you. Will you stay with me?"

He nodded, his voice taut. "I will."

She kissed him one last time, then stared up into his eyes.

"It's not up to me," he reminded her. "But I'll pray that we can be together."

She leaned into his chest, hearing his heartbeat. "I will, too. I will pray harder than I ever have before."

CHAPTER TWENTY-ONE

ux and Vira were on the west side of the city. Unlike Naomi and Ferrin, neither of them had ever been to Le'Gar. Strolling through the streets was mystical to Hux, and he couldn't stop from glancing up at the gargoyles every two minutes to make sure they weren't staring directly at him.

"They aren't going to eat you alive," Vira said, watching him. "They're frozen to their places."

"I wouldn't be surprised if they knew about my treason and decided it would be a grand idea to gouge my eyes out with their talons."

"Graves, Hux." Vira groaned through a laugh. "You think they'd be against you for doing what is right?"

"We know it was right. But do they?"

Vira pointed a finger up at the stone beasts. "They're on Naomi's side, and so are you, which means they're on your side."

He cast his attention to a fountain in the middle of the intersection. "I can't help but think I'm the only one who shouldn't be here."

"What? Why do you believe that?"

Hux lifted his empty left hand. "I'm solely human. And the rest of you aren't. I may have good intentions, but how am I useful?"

"Has this been bothering you?" Vira asked.

"I wouldn't say I'm bothered. It's just a constant thought."

"Well, cast that thought away," she demanded. "Because you're wrong. Who ever said you had to be something other than human to be great?"

He put on a sarcastic smirk. "Almost everyone."

"King Leeland saw something great in you."

"King Leeland is a fool," said Hux, "and I betrayed him."

Vira rolled her eyes and walked toward the stone fountain. "Why are you being so hard on yourself?"

Hux stayed put, watching Vira wander away from him. "Because I couldn't do anything to save you," he said to himself.

But Vira turned back toward him. "I heard that. I felt that."

"So there it is," he admitted. "I had to watch you lie there, dying in Ferrin's arms, and I couldn't do anything but ask you to keep holding on."

Vira rubbed her temples and closed her eyes. "What is it with you and having to do something to prove yourself?"

"I'm not trying to prove myself." He took a heavy step toward her. "I'm only attempting to do what I do best: protect. And I feel that I can't do that."

She closed the gap between them to stand almost chest to chest. "Why is it such a bad thing if you aren't the strongest wolf in the pack?"

He glared. "Forget it." He moved to the side and brushed past her shoulder, but Vira stepped in front of him. They bumped together and he let out an exasperated breath. "Stop, Vira. I don't want to have this conversation. We're out here to search the city, not to argue."

"We aren't arguing. Tell me why protecting me matters so much to you? For once in your life, Hux, explain how you're feeling."

"I've explained plenty to you. But you still don't understand."

"I'm trying to understand."

"Don't you see?" He waved a hand between them. "We are too equal. You will never need me."

"What?"

Hux's words came out stronger. "You will never need me."

Vira watched his eyes falter as she summoned up a response. "Yes, I will. I do."

"You don't have to lie to me," he scoffed. "I'm tired of lies."

"You're angry at me."

"Oh," he laughed. "I'm not angry at *you*. I'm angry at *myself*. For being nothing but a paralytic treasonist."

"Hux," Vira snapped. "Where is this coming from?"

But then she saw the way his left fist hung clenched at his side, and the way his shoulders sagged farther forward than they ever had. And his eyes. They were dark.

"Hux," she said with more fervor. "Wake up."

"What do you think I'm doing, sleepwalking?"

She grabbed his shoulders and gave him a shake. "Hux! It's Calamity. It's toying with you. Please, wake up."

"Let go of me, witch," he growled.

"For graves' sake," Vira hissed right back. "Look at me. Look."

He did, but his eyes still held their shadow.

"Hey," she shifted her tone, going softer. "I need you right now. Please? You don't think I need you, but I've been so alone for years, and when you sent a messenger saying you needed my help, I was overjoyed. Because I knew we are kindred spirits. You told me you were beginning to love me. Is that still true?"

The shadow flitted from his eyes. "What?"

"You said you were beginning to love me when we were young. I said, is that still true?"

"I—" He blinked. "Vira?"

She stood right at his face, her hands still on his shoulders.

He furrowed his brows. "Did I black out? I feel like I blacked out."

Vira's voice was stuck in the back of her throat. "Yes. Yes, you blacked out. It happened to Millie once, too. Calamity is attempting to move inside your mind."

"Oh." Hux ran his fingers through his beard. "What was I saying? Or were you saying something?"

Vira shook her head. "I was just begging you to wake up." She let go of his shoulders and tilted her head toward the fountain. "Come with me."

"To the fountain?"

"Yes." The way she said it sounded strangled to Hux, like she was forcing a conversation change.

He walked shoulder to shoulder with her to the circular fountain. In the center were two statues. One was a young girl, leaping on one foot and reaching upward as if to catch something. The statue next to her was a young boy, holding an open book in one hand, while his other hand sat open like he was waiting for a bird to land in his palm.

Hux studied Vira. "Are you sure I didn't say anything strange? You look disturbed."

"Hux, you just—"

But her voice fell away with the sound of cracking and a sudden jolt. The world blurred before Hux's eyes as if he were in a drunken sprint and the ground was no longer beneath him. He began to fall, and the sky lay on its side.

The world was tipping again.

"Vira!" Hux screamed.

Vira grasped through the air, trying to get ahold of something.

Then Hux's hand clamped around her bicep as he clung to the fountain.

"I got you," he shouted, as objects fell downward all around them.

Vira closed her eyes, not daring to see what the objects were. If she was falling, others were falling, too. She didn't want to see that.

Hux's hand shook as he clung desperately to her arm.

"It will right itself!" she called up to him. "Keep holding, keep holding." She squeezed her eyes closed again, and searched for any energy in the chaotic space that she could grasp onto, and wrap around Hux to give him strength. But her own powers were spiraling in the midst of her adrenaline. "Focus," she whispered to herself. "Calm. Calm."

Then Hux's grip tightened. Vira shot her eyes open. She hadn't been able to grasp any energy. Hux's extra strength was his own. Out of his own desperation, he was holding fast. *A human,* she thought, as she hung suspended over the sky, *could have as much power as me if they love something enough.*

CHAPTER TWENTY-TWO

When Thãen tipped, Naomi had a split second to grab onto the horn of the beast gargoyle. Her feet swung out from under her and only the tips of her fingers made contact with the stone horn. The grip wasn't secure enough, and she fell.

But Ferrin's hand caught her sleeve as he held onto the roof's ledge.

Suspended over the city, Naomi saw the veins on Ferrin's neck and face bulging. She kicked her feet, attempting to swing herself back up.

"No!" Ferrin ordered. "Don't move. I'm—I'm losing grip."

Then Naomi dared to look down. The city lay on its side. Particles of dirt and loose foliage from the mountains sailed down toward the curve of the world, where the sky met the sea. It was just as her father had said. One day Thãen would roll like a marble into the palm of Calamity. It was beginning to happen.

"Ferrin," Naomi shouted, "you can't hold us both."

"I am holding us both," he wheezed. "Just wait. Thãen will tip back like it did before."

As if to mock him, the world rolled even further, the sea now at Naomi's feet, miles below.

"Drop me," she ordered.

"*What?*"

"I said drop me!"

"You're crazy!" he hollered.

"You're losing grip!" she screamed, watching his fingers slide little by little off her sleeve. "Drop me now and I'll land in the sea."

Though they hung upside down and the world lay inside out, Naomi was able to keep contact with Ferrin's eyes.

"Please don't make me do this," he begged, straining.

The world shifted again, rocking slightly.

Panic surged through Naomi's chest. "If you don't drop me now, you may lose your hold when the mountain is at my feet! Or worse, the stone street! Let go, Ferrin!"

His face contorted with pain. "Graves. I'll find you."

"I know. Now let me go."

And with his eyes closed, he released her.

CHAPTER TWENTY-THREE

The fall wasn't the worst part. It was the smack against the ocean's surface that stung Naomi like a thousand whips.

Be nice to me, she had prayed as she fell. And all things considered, the Desarian Sea was nice to her. It didn't kill her upon impact.

She sank below the surface, so far that when she finally stopped moving downward, all the air in her lungs had run out. She pulled herself upward, but the little ground she gained made no difference. She would never make it to the surface.

Take me to the top! she thought through a blurred mind. *I demand you to surface me!*

The water rumbled beneath her, and out of the dark, black, deep morphed an underwater wave. It roared upward and lifted her.

Her vision was black. Her lungs were ice cold. But when her head broke through the surface of the water, a furious gasp erupted from her and her eyes shot open to see bright sunlight and a cloudless sky. The world was right back where it should be, as if nothing had ever happened.

She trod water and coughed and gagged. "There's still time," she gasped to herself. "It's not over."

Then she began to swim. She could see the landmass that was Le'Gar in the distance, but it was far. Even so, she pulled herself that way. Her arms burned with each stroke and her heart beat like a walloping sledgehammer.

"I need to end this," she recited over and over. "I can end this. I need to end this."

The tide pulled her farther out as she swam in. Any effort she gave was taken away and swallowed by the waves.

"Take me to shore!" she screamed with water flying off her lip.

A deep ache hummed through her bones as the tide suddenly shifted. This time, when she swam, there was no resistance, but fatigue overwhelmed her. Controlling the sea was different than controlling land. The sea itself was energy, and it cost her.

Easing up, she let the sea move more freely, and she found that she could strike a balance between controlling the waters and swimming on her own. Give and take. If she used her powers too much, it sapped her strength. But there was a healthy balance. A right way. And she found it.

The mountains in the distance were growing larger now. It was swim or drown.

And she didn't cross the Desarian Sea years ago only to be swallowed by it now.

CHAPTER TWENTY-FOUR

Ferrin skirted debris as he sprinted through the streets of Le'Gar. The city was in shambles. Any item that had been loose when the world tipped littered the roads. Books, market carts, flowers, store signs, people. There were people. *Bodies crushed.* If he wanted to get Naomi back, he had to turn a blind eye to the disaster around him. Ignore the terrified Le'Garians flooding out of the buildings to inspect the damage.

Ferrin leapt over a chunk of stone that had fallen from a building and smashed right into a hefty man. He caught himself by clinging to the man's arms and gasped in relief when he realized it was Hux. "Thank Protection. I need your help."

Hux held him up, staring at him with penetrating, questioning eyes. "Are you alright? Are you hurt? Where—"

"Naomi fell into the sea," Ferrin blurted out. "From the top of the roof. She made me let her go, I didn't want to, I swear Hux, I didn't want to."

Suddenly the panic and pain he was feeling made ugly sense to Ferrin. Yes, he was worried about the state Naomi was now in, but a sickeningly familiar stab of hatred for himself socked him in the gut. He'd watched Oliver sail off the roof and meet his death in the streets, a murder that Ferrin took the blame for. Could it be that he had failed yet again in such a similar way? Only this time he wasn't watching the woman he loved do the killing. The woman he had grown to love was the victim.

"Of course you didn't want to," Hux barked, but somehow exposed a calming undertone. "We'll find her."

Vira appeared from behind Hux, her hair a mess and her face dotted with sweat. "Can you find her with your mind?"

Ferrin shut his eyes and took deep, soothing breaths. He shoved aside all the sounds in the real world and tried to focus on the soulful part of his mind, the part where the Magnificent in him lived. But to no avail. He could find no sound of Naomi's voice and no soft energy of her presence. But another presence pierced into his brain with a fiery entrance. Estell.

"Please, no," Ferrin whispered.

"What is it?" Vira snapped. "Where is Naomi?"

"It's not her I'm feeling," he muttered, looking around frantically. "Estell. She's in Le'Gar."

"It was only a matter of time," Vira sorrowfully admitted. "She won't stop until she finds Naomi." Vira put a hand on both men's shoulders and shoved them in the direction of Eli's house.

"Then we need to find her first," Ferrin demanded, as he dodged a mess of fruits and meats that had been splattered and strewn about the street. "I know Estell will kill her. Just like she did Oliver."

"She won't," Hux assured. "Because Naomi's life isn't solely in your hands or in Eli's. She's in all of ours, and we'll fight to the death to keep her safe."

Ferrin swallowed tears as he understood the truth in Hux's

words. *I'm not alone*, he finally accepted. *The weight doesn't fall entirely on me.*

"Move aside," Vira hissed, shoving the men off the street and into a nook in the stone buildings.

Ferrin staggered as he and Hux bumped into each other, and Vira threw her cloak around them both. The sound of hooves galloped by, and Estell's presence swelled in Ferrin's head.

Vira waited for the horses to disappear down the street before she drew her cloak back, letting Ferrin and Hux back out into the sunlight.

"Estell and Saul," Vira explained with regret. "They're heading to the King's cathedral. They will tell King Tal that Naomi is here."

"Graves," Ferrin whispered. "We're running out of time."

"We are," Vira downheartedly agreed. "We need to find her fast. Maybe Eli can feel her location."

"Then let's make haste," Ferrin ordered, turning toward Eli's house. "She needs us."

And I need her.

CHAPTER TWENTY-FIVE

Saul guided his horse up to the front steps of the King's cathedral, then reined in and jumped to the ground with Estell at his heels. Casting a quick glance over his shoulder, he eyed the scrape that covered half of her face. She didn't act like she was in pain. She simply tucked her shiny hair behind her ear and kept her chin held high. Saul was impressed that a woman could be crushed by a horse as the world tipped, only to rise and keep moving like nothing had happened. He gritted his teeth repeatedly to swallow the nauseating pain from his dislocated shoulder. But the world's tip itself didn't scare him. It only gave him hope that Calamity was winning.

Estell touched his shoulder as they ascended the front stone stairs. "Remember," she whispered, "even though King Tal wants Naomi dead, it may not be because he's fighting for Calamity. Humanity changes sides easily," she added. "He may be straddling the line of his old self and a new self. We are so close to wiping Naomi Massoud from this world. So close to eliminating the weapon that she is. We shouldn't blindly trust King Tal. He could stop us from killing Naomi. We must kill Naomi."

"And we will," Saul assured her. " But let me do the talking. I know King Tal the best. I know his weaknesses."

As soon as Saul and Estell thundered through the front double doors of the King's cathedral and into the towering foyer, guards and castle hands held their swords up in defense, only to lower them at once when they recognized Saul. Saul had been King Tal's Lead Rider and was highly respected in Le'Gar. Apparently he still held their respect.

"We must speak to the King," Saul ordered, holding his hands up. "We know how to stop the world from tipping. We know where the last living Massoud is."

The guards rushed around, jostling Saul and Estell into the empty throne hall, where they waited in the silence while King Tal was fetched.

Tal entered the throne hall, his arms bruised and scraped, his robe hanging at the crooks of his arms. He limped toward Saul and Estell, staring blankly at his lost Rider.

"You're unwell," Saul pointed out through a frown. "Do you need to sit down?"

"No, no, I do not need to sit down!" Tal said. "My city is flipping upside down and bodies are lying in the streets! And where have you been?" He waved a shaking hand at Estell. "Who is this? Did you forget your mission? The quill, Saul! The Massoud! Our people are in danger!"

"Sir," Saul interjected. "We're here to help you. I've been tracking down a way to end this, just as you requested." He shrugged a shoulder at Estell. "This is Estell. She's a golden witch, and she's been using her powers to help me track down the one we seek. Naomi Massoud is the girl's name, and she's here in Le'Gar."

Tal zeroed in on the golden witch in front of him. "Estell. Bold of you to use the same name as the one you used years ago when you worked for my great-grandfather."

She shifted, appearing uncomfortable. "So you know who I am."

"I know who you are," Tal confirmed, "and I know what you've done. I know you were the one who killed Oliver Massoud."

Estell fluttered her eyes upward at the King. "Then you know I'm on your side."

Saul's heart hammered. In a confused frenzy, his mind struggled to choose which direction to take. Estell worked for his family in the past, but his family worked for Calamity even then, and that meant Estell should assume Tal still does work for Calamity. Tal had one foot on Calamity's side and one foot on the Massoud's side, and he needed to deal his cards just right to keep both Calamity and Estell on his side.

"Then you're welcome here," Tal stated, suppressing a rising urge to cast her out. "I stand with my family's mission."

Saul looked from King Tal to Estell and back again, and said, "All this time, sir? You've been riding in Calamity's palm? I've always thought your orders throughout the years were influenced by your want to keep Le'Gar a safe place. When you sent us Riders out to find the golden quill, I thought it was because you wanted to keep the war between the gods at bay, but now I see I was mistaken. You've been working for Calamity the whole time, haven't you?"

Tal fought to keep his face still, then nodded. It seemed to him that Saul had made an allegiance to Calamity. If Saul was working with Estell and they were both eager to find the Massoud, they had to be working for Calamity. Tal needed to keep Saul and Estell thinking he was still working with Calamity. He needed *Calamity* to believe he was still working for it.

"I felt Naomi's presence here," Estell revealed. "She's in your city, though she feels faraway at the present moment. It's possible the tip tossed her out. Even so, she will be back."

Tal nodded again. "I need to inspect the city," he said, changing course. "I am a disciple of Calamity, but I am also a king. It would be unwise of me to turn a blind eye to my people in a devastating time. Especially if I want to keep my alliance with Calamity hidden."

Estell cocked her head to the side and gazed at Tal. "What is Calamity's real name?"

"That's something you should know," Tal spat. "If you're truly a disciple, that is." He crossed his arms. "You question me, yet I can question you, too."

"Hilith," she hissed. "Now prove your alliance."

Tal's pulse quickened, but his lie came quicker. "I murdered my father for the sake of keeping our alliance with Calamity hidden."

Saul's eyes flew open wide. "Sir, when?"

"While you were gone," Tal deadpanned. "And it meant nothing to me. Anything for Hilith."

Estell nodded and bit her lip as she smiled. "I see the darkness on you. Now give us the official order to sweep the city and put an end to this madness. We can have Naomi Massoud murdered by morning."

"*In* the morning," he corrected. "We won't begin our search for Naomi until dawn. I told you already, I am still a king. I must act as my people expect me to act." He turned to Saul. "Take up your old living quarters in the Riders' hall. Take the witch with you."

"The witch's name is Estell."

Tal pointed to his own face. "I don't care. All I care about is finding Naomi Massoud and her dreaded quill. Don't show your face to anyone else, and for goodness sake don't leave the cathedral. We don't want to give Naomi a heads-up that we're coming."

CHAPTER TWENTY-SIX

Vira flew through the door to Eli's home first. She fled across the floor to where Deirdre had Millicent propped up on the couch as she bandaged the girl's arms and legs, which were full of cuts and bruises.

Dropping to her knees, Vira pulled her daughter into her arms. "Are you alright? I'm so sorry I was gone."

"It's okay, Mum," Millicent reassured in a muffled breath against Vira's shoulder.

Then the back of the fireplace slid open and Eli stepped out of the hidden tunnel, blood running down the side of his face. He blinked when he saw the disastrous state of his home, but quickly shifted his focus to the others in front of him. "Where is Naomi?"

Ferrin stepped forward, sweat soaking his shirt from sprinting through the streets. "The wound on your head needs tending." He pointed to Eli's blood. "Come here."

Eli's eyes crinkled, but he didn't smile. "No, Fin, I'll be alright. I don't need the healing. Where is Naomi?"

"We lost her in the sea when the world flipped," Ferrin

choked. "And I can't feel her. Can you feel her, Eli? You've always been stronger than me."

Hux hung his head. "Graves, don't tell me she's dead."

"Don't even say that," Ferrin begged. "It can't be."

"It may not be so," Eli comforted. "Come here."

Ferrin stepped forward so that he was face-to-face with Eli.

"Do you remember what I once told you about a Magnificent and the limit of their powers?" Eli quizzed.

And though it had been years and years ago, Ferrin did remember. "That a Magnificent is only as powerful as those around him," he recited. "So a Magnificent who works alone is limited by himself, but a Magnificent in the company of other Magnificents has the potential to elevate beyond their normal reach."

"Precisely," Eli affirmed. "Let's find her together."

Vira lifted her face from Millicent's little body and watched as Eli placed his hands on the sides of Ferrin's head. Both Magnificents leaned in until their foreheads touched.

Ferrin stood tense, but he lifted his own hands and rested them on the sides of Eli's face.

"We can do this, young Mag," Eli reassured. "Though we haven't worked together for years, we are still familiar with each other, yes?"

Ferrin nodded against Eli's head. "Yes."

"Let Mavelic guide you," Eli instructed, as he shut his eyes. "He will direct your thoughts."

Ferrin swallowed and forced his own eyes closed. His mind felt empty and heavy as he began to search, but a speck of light in his mind poked through. A pathway. A pinprick of hope. He followed it, and soon the echo of Eli's thoughts were in his head.

Naomi, Eli's thoughts called out. *Naomi Massoud. I'm seeking Naomi Massoud.*

"I see her," Ferrin whispered, choking down the emotion that welled in his throat. "I see her in the Desarian Sea, but she's too far out. All I can see is water in every direction."

Eli kept his hands clamped to Ferrin's head. "I see her too. She's alive."

Ferrin's eyes remained closed and he had blocked out everyone else in the room. "She's swimming, but in what direction? How will we know where on the shore she will end up?"

A loud whooshing noise flooded Ferrin's ears as Eli let go and stepped back. The two Magnificents stood staring at each other, and became aware now of the other eyes in the room that watched them.

"She's alive then?" Hux pried, moving a step closer to them.

"Yes," Eli confirmed, his voice falling flat. He glanced out the small front window. "But night is falling. She won't be able to see the shore in the dark."

"Then we need to go." Ferrin charged toward the door.

Eli grabbed Ferrin's shoulder. "Wait."

"I'm not waiting," he protested.

Eli held his hand up. "I'm saying 'wait' as in 'wait for me.' I'm going with you."

"Oh. Sorry."

Turning, Eli rummaged around the disheveled room in search of his long cloak.

"I will go, too," Hux piped up.

Ferrin nodded without question. "Of course."

Vira still held onto Millicent. "I need to stay here with her. I can't—I can't leave her. Another shift could happen."

Deirdre stood and gathered the first aid supplies. "Vira and I will keep Millicent here. You three, go. Get our girl back."

CHAPTER TWENTY-SEVEN

Naomi knew now how it felt to be drained of power. She could only control the sea for so long before exhaustion overtook her and threatened to swallow her whole. The shore was visible, but she feared she would drown before she had the strength to reach it.

Please just help me, she prayed to the sea, searching for her elusive powers.

A wave washed over her, giving her a gentle push. Then another and another. Every time a wave came, Naomi swam, riding with its help.

The shore grew closer as the world grew darker. Nightfall was coming. Every wave inched Naomi closer to land ever so slowly. When her powers started to feel drained, she floated, regaining what little energy she could. She did this for what felt like eternity. The little blip of land ahead was still so far, and when the stars started to appear, Naomi grew desperate.

With a pulse of ambition, Naomi drove her arms forward and began to swim a steady stroke. She would not be left for dead in the sea. Even when her muscles burned and her breathing became labored, she kept going. It was slow...so slow.

Another wave lapped up against her and washed over her ears.

Let it flow, it whispered.

Then another wave.

Let it flow.

Naomi closed her eyes and listened to nature's voice. *Let it flow* was the first thing nature ever said to her, and she still didn't know what it meant, but right now she took it as encouragement from nature. If she could just flow with the sea, as if she were a part of it, she would reach the shore. She was sure of it.

Then Naomi's feet touched the pebbly bottom of the sea. Her heart welled with relief as she let her legs take over. As she dragged herself toward shore, the sea's whispers hissed behind her.

Let it flow.

She wanted to beg the sea to tell her what it meant, but she only had energy to keep breathing.

Le'Gar sat in the distance, lit with specks of light from its torches, but the beach before her was dark. Black and empty.

Naomi fell to her knees on the sand. Exhausted. She collapsed, lying there, shivering and panting. She closed her eyes and with the last bit of her energy, her mind cried out for Ferrin.

Please find me. I need you. I have nothing left.

She closed her eyes and lay unmoving. Then the dream came, the one she and Ferrin shared and had seen many times before.

She is in Le'Gar, at the King's cathedral, in the throne room, when the doors are thrown open and King Tal falls through them, his throat sliced. The Hand of Calamity, a black, shadowy hand, is close behind, blooming into the room, dark smoke crawling over the ceiling, overtaking the room. Naomi stands, unmoving, but in her mind, she calls out to Ferrin. She's been in this dream before, and every time, Ferrin appears in the doorway to the throne room. Suddenly he's there, pointing at her.

"Omi, look out," he says, but with blank eyes. "Someone's there."

And the dream slows. Everything moves as if stuck in molasses. Naomi turns around.

Behind her is the face of King Tal. He is shouting at her. His mouth is open in alarm and his arm is raised, pointing at her. He is saying something, but his words sound like they are underwater.

Naomi takes a step toward him, but before her lays the dead and bleeding King Tal.

There are two Tals. One dead. One still alive and shouting at her. This is where her dream ended before, but this time she sees more, though she cannot hear him.

"What are you saying? she asks him. "What are you telling me?"

She reaches toward him. Her fingers touch nothing visible, then she feels something solid, cold. A glass wall is between them that shatters a moment later. His words are suddenly crystal clear.

"Naomi! It's Estell!" Tal is screaming. "She's here for you, Naomi. She's coming! She's coming!"

The dream begins to quickly fade from the edges. Blackness spins in front of Naomi's face like a vortex and she looks from live Tal, to dead Tal, to live Tal again. There are two of them before her. They are the same King Tal, each who has chosen a different path. Dead Tal chose to keep serving Calamity, but live Tal chose to protect Naomi. Before she can ask why, the dream fades, leaving behind the single question: which foretold path would King Tal of Le'Gar choose?

CHAPTER TWENTY-EIGHT

King Tal's eyes shot open. Sweat covered every inch of his body. The dream he just had still lingered in his mind.

He'd seen his own death. He watched his dying self tumbling through the doors of his throne room, his throat slit before he fell to the floor, his life bleeding out of him. Naomi stood inside, staring at him. She glanced up as The Dark Hand of Calamity towered over her. She showed no emotion, no fear. In a dark corner of the throne room stood Estell. She morphed out of the shadows like a black cat and wore a senile grin. Her gaze was fixated on Naomi, and all Tal could think to do was to warn her, to scream.

"Naomi! It's Estell! She's here for you, Naomi! She's coming! She's coming!"

Now, sitting in his bed, he knew beyond a doubt that the dream meant something. The cold sweat he woke with was fading. He took a deep breath, then looked to the window.

It was still night outside, but he felt as if the streets below were stirring. Not because he was capable of actually feeling such things, like a golden witch or a Magnificent, but because a force was overpowering him, something that sank into his being. It was enough to draw him out of bed and to the window, creeping so he didn't wake his wife.

He pulled the curtains aside and peered down at the street below. Lanterns lined the stone road below, but everything else was laden in black.

Until a female figure with stark white hair floated into view, running up the street.

Estell.

She had a quiver and bow slung on her back and a sword at her side. Tal knew she was leaving the cathedral to begin her search for Naomi, even though he told her and Saul that they would hunt for Naomi in the morning.

Tal felt panic drop into his stomach like a stone. He had made up his mind. The consequences of turning on Calamity would be severe, but he would try to play the game as long as possible. He couldn't let anything bad happen to Naomi. If Naomi could bring an end to Calamity's torture, Tal wanted her to do so. Calamity had controlled Tal and his family for long enough, and he wanted out. He wanted a taste of the light, and he wanted his daughters to live free of Calamity's influence. But to help Naomi, Tal would have to keep Calamity thinking he was still a disciple. Lying to a god was risky, but Tal was willing to take that risk. He may be tainted by his previous service to Calamity, but all of his good wasn't lost. There was enough good left to make a difference.

CHAPTER TWENTY-NINE

Naomi came to on the beach, her cheek plastered against the sand. The first hint of dawn was on the horizon. She blinked, attempting to clear her vision. She was too exhausted to move.

A man's feet appeared in her line of vision, attached to a pair of legs striding toward her. He walked calmly, with purpose. A long cloak flowed to the back of his knees. Relief swept over her. *Ferrin.*

The feet neared her then stopped.

Naomi tried to sit up, fighting against the dizziness in her head, but she could only lie propped on an elbow while she waited for the dizziness to stop. Her stomach felt sick from it. She tried to control her breathing so she wouldn't be sick, and then she slowly raised her gaze to the man standing over her.

King Tal.

For a moment they merely stared at each other. King Tal looking down, Naomi looking up.

Then she sat up. "If you came here to stop me, I'll call up the sea to swallow you," she said unshaking.

He glanced at the sea, as if judging whether Naomi really could control it or not.

"I can do that," she assured. "I can let the sea take you."

Tal stood still, thoughtful, then offered her his hand. "Here. Get up." After she stood and was steady, he said, "I came here to tell you one thing. I want you to listen."

Naomi thought about her dream. About how there was a version of Tal that helped her. "I'm listening?" she said, short.

He looked her dead in the eyes. "You're a part of Calamity."

She scowled. "No. You lie. I'm not. You're only trying to trick me."

"I do not lie," he snapped. "Listen. Calamity wants you to know that you are a part of it. That's what *it* wants you to know." He paused, watching her.

That's what it wants you to know. Naomi shook her head, believing what he said impossible, but the way Tal said it didn't sit right with her. As if Tal wanted her to know this for a different reason.

"So what does that mean?" she asked slowly.

Tal shrugged. "I don't know. I only know what matters at this moment is that you know." He took a step toward her. "That you know this before you die," he threatened.

Naomi stepped back.

"I'm here to kill you," he said, with a slight tremble but did not move closer. He seemed frightened. Or unsure

Naomi tensed her fingers. She would unleash the sea on him

"So kill me," she tested.

He reached for the dagger at his hip. "I will if you don't stop me."

There was a slight change in his tone, as if he was tormenting her like prey, but she could read past his eyes. He was asking her to stop him. She knew Tal worked for Calamity.

She knew he had to tread carefully. Then she understood. He *had* to try to kill her right now. Otherwise, Calamity would kill him.

She curled her fingers into her palms and let the twitch of a smile show. "Let it flow."

He frowned. "What?"

"It's a phrase," she said nonchalantly. "One that I think can defeat you and Calamity."

Tal's eyes widened, realizing she was offering him a piece of information in return.

"Not if I kill you first," he thundered, acting his part.

Naomi raised her fists. "Good luck."

Then stepping away, she uncurled her fingers and called forth a towering wave.

He hesitated too long. Water slammed onto the beach and crashed over Tal as he pulled his dagger.

Then she ran.

CHAPTER THIRTY

Naomi ran up the slope of the mountain, into the pines leading to the city. Her mind reeled with the idea that Tal wanted to help her. And he thought telling her that she was a part of Calamity would somehow help her. But why? How could it possibly be a good thing to be a part of a malevolent god? How could knowing that be an advantage?

The white light of dawn shone through the trees as Naomi hiked toward Le'Gar. Her clothes were drenched, her body ached. She'd never felt the want to see the city streets like she did now. And she was almost there. The outskirts of the city were nearly visible. But a sound made her stop.

Like leaves tumbling, but there was no wind.

Naomi tensed, digging deep to where her powers were refueling. She spun, looking behind her, but the woods were empty. Only when she turned back around did her heart fly out of her chest. In front of her stood Estell.

"You should have kept your back to me," Estell sneered, holding a sword out in front of her. "I could have lobbed off your head effortlessly."

Naomi stood tall. "Try."

Without hesitation, Estell swung the sword.

Naomi lunged to the side and stumbled. Estell was on her before she could regain her balance. They both collapsed to the forest floor, the sword against Naomi's neck.

"It's so easy," Estell taunted with a grin. "You're a naive little thing."

Naomi threw her arms to the side and felt the power of the ground beneath her. She called forth a tornado of dirt, knocking Estell off of her.

Estell rolled with the cloud of dust, nearly losing hold of her sword. Naomi jumped to her feet and sent the roots of a tree crawling toward the golden witch. The roots reached for Estell's ankles, but she slashed at them with her blade, cutting her loose.

A physical pain struck Naomi in her chest. So much so that she fell to her knees. Every time Estell wounded a root, Naomi felt the blow.

Estell stopped, sneering at Naomi's posture. "Ah. I see your powers have a limit." She sliced another root and laughed when Naomi clutched her chest.

Naomi gritted her teeth and breathed through the pain. She let go of her control over the roots and the feeling of being stabbed left.

Estell ran over to Naomi and held her sword under her chin. "Time's up."

Naomi glanced up. Maybe Estell was right. She had nothing left to give. The sea had drained her. Her fatigue now was paralyzing. She couldn't get up and run. She couldn't fight. She was at the mercy of Estell's sword.

"Fine," Naomi accepted, breathing heavy. She kept her eyes trained on Estell, but in the distance, three men appeared. Naomi's heart leapt. She knew those three men. They were *her* men. And if she could distract Estell long enough, she knew the men would save her. "Let me tell you one thing."

Estell squinted, staring down. "What?"

Naomi tried to think of something that would throw Estell off the most. Something that could maybe give Naomi a moment to run toward Ferrin, Eli, and Hux, who were silently approaching. "You thought you destroyed Ferrin, but you didn't. He found happiness again. With me."

Estell's lips wavered. The sword lowered for a fraction of a second. Naomi took that second to dart. But she wasn't fast enough. Estell's sword sliced her bicep. Naomi grabbed the wound and felt warm blood seep through her fingers.

When Estell turned to finish her off, Hux was already there. He plowed his massive body into her and she dropped her sword and fell to the ground where Hux held her down.

Naomi looked down. The sword had sliced her bicep, and blood seeped down her arm and covered her hand. But it wasn't red. It was black.

Ferrin wrapped his cloak around her arm, trying to stop the bleeding, but she knew he was also trying to hide the color. "I've got you," he promised her. "We've got you."

Hux rolled off of Estell as Eli held her in place with an invisible force. She lay on her back in the most helpless position. Eli walked toward her, fury showing within every ounce of his being. When he stood over her, Naomi feared he might kill her on the spot, but he only looked down.

"So what will you do with me?" she taunted in a sing-song voice. "Try to convert me?"

"Kill her," Hux boomed. "She deserves to die."

Eli held up a hand. "She'll come with us. A prisoner."

Estell pouted. "That's no fun. I'm not coming." She shifted her eyes to Naomi. "Calamity already knows the Massoud is here. It's coming for Le'Gar next, and its own worst enemy is itself. You don't stand a chance."

"We'll take our chances," Ferrin hissed. "I'd rather die than serve it."

"You will die," Estell said, almost sad. "And I'm sorry that you will." She blinked. "Look at the woman you've fallen in love with. She's dark. She isn't the saint you think she is."

Naomi closed her eyes, not wanting to look at the thing Estell was referring to.

Her blood, which was seeping through his cloak, staining it black.

Estell smiled again. "Now I say farewell, but I'll see you soon." She let out a loud cackle. Her open mouth revealed a thick swarm of flies that grew as they flew upward and then engulfed her. In a flash she was gone.

"What kind of sorcery was that?" Hux said, aghast.

Eli stood staring at the spot where Estell had been. "Dark sorcery. She has joined with Calamity."

"We need to get Naomi back so I can fully heal this wound," Ferrin said, keeping his arms around her.

Hux and Eli stared at Naomi, her arm covered with Ferrin's cloak.

"Let me see it," Eli ordered gently.

Naomi shook her head, tears glistening her eyes. "No. Please. No."

Eli took a tender step forward. "Let me see. So I know it's true."

"It's true," Naomi cried softly. "Even King Tal told me. I'm a part of Calamity."

Ferrin frowned at her. "King Tal? When?"

"He found me on the beach," Naomi revealed. "He told me. He said I had to know, before he purposely stalled in killing me, giving me enough time to send a wave over him and get away."

Eli nodded knowingly. "Perhaps our king is second guessing his alliance."

"Maybe," Naomi agreed. "But that doesn't change the fact that I'm filled with something dark."

Ferrin peeled the cloak back to check the wound. The bleeding was slowing and red blood was now mixed with the black. He held a hand over the gash and sent a wave of healing power into her.

Naomi tried to pull her arm away, afraid that if he touched her dark blood he would turn evil. But the warmth from his healing was too powerful. The bleeding slowed to a stop, even though the gash remained.

Ferrin brought his eyes to hers. "Your decisions make you who you are." He took her hand, letting the sticky black blood coat his own fingers. "Not your flesh and bone. Or blood. And I know you. I wanted to hate you. I tried to hate you. But I grew to love you instead. You're not meant for something evil."

She swallowed, closing her eyes. "But something dark is inside of me. What if it wins in the end?"

Ferrin was quiet for a moment. "I'll still love you."

CHAPTER THIRTY-ONE

In the early hours of the morning, King Tal swam back to shore, then made it home, where he hid out in his chambers. His wife was in the galley with his daughters, having a usual morning, but he was having quite the opposite.

The note from his father still sat snug against his chest beneath his shirt. He'd kept it close to him every day, in fear that if someone were to find it, they'd discover his secret. But now he pulled it out and read it over again.

"Insert the key but warn Le'Gar. Ring the bell. Let—"

Tal stared. The last word. Let. The note ended abruptly. It had been unfinished. But Naomi had said it to him on the shores.

Let it flow.

But what did it mean? Let what flow?

He started running through ideas in his head. What are things that flow? Blood and water. But there are so many types of water. Lakes, oceans, waterfalls, creeks, rivers.

His head snapped up.

There was a strange legend about the rivers in Raina. Their

rivers were red, and there was talk that they were red from ink. Ink also flowed.

In one quick stride, King Tal was at his window. He looked down and saw the streets filling with their morning crowd. Tal had to work quickly. He felt that time was not on his side.

Drawing his cloak closed, he headed to the hall, quietly, easily, as if everything were normal, avoiding exchanging looks with the guards as he passed through the cathedral and out into the open air.

With his eyes cast low and head bowed, he made for Deirdre's library. He knew she had what he was looking for.

He was almost to the library's steps when a sharp pain struck him in the sternum. He stumbled, clutching at his chest. For a moment he stopped to breathe in the shadows of an alley-way. Sweat beaded on his forehead as he blinked away the pain.

It was as he feared.

Calamity was beginning to realize he was working against it.

It would only be a matter of time before Calamity killed him. Just like it killed his father.

But Tal sucked in a deep breath and stepped out into the street again. He would do as much as he could before Calamity destroyed him. His family's service to The Dark Hand would end with him.

CHAPTER THIRTY-TWO

Naomi sat on the bed in the back room of Eli's home. Ferrin knelt in front of her, wiping up the blood that caked her arm. She kept her eyes away from him and the blood. The black blood. When she looked at it, she grew upset.

Hushed whispers drifted under the door from the living room, where Hux and Eli told Vira and Deirdre what happened. Naomi heard Vira say Estell would come back to finish off Naomi. Hux regretted they hadn't killed Estell before she could get away in a cloud of black magic. But the next whispers were about Naomi. About her black blood and what it meant.

Ferrin glanced up at Naomi as he used another warm cloth to scrub away the last remaining spots of black. "Don't worry about what they're saying. No one questions your loyalty."

"I question me," Naomi whispered.

"Have you known about the color of your blood this whole time?"

Naomi shook her head. "My blood has always been red. Always. Why is it changing now?"

Ferrin ran a finger over the place where the wound once

was, making sure he had healed it closed. "Perhaps your true self lay dormant, just like your powers. Maybe your blood is a part of your awakening."

"What am I, then?"

"You're something otherworldly," he answered.

"Am I a god?" Naomi cringed.

"It's a valid question," Ferrin reassured. "And Brahm back in Mira Isla seemed to think that you were. But Deirdre said your bloodline was created by Protection." He sat on the bed next to her. "So that would make you what? Offspring of the gods? A pawn?" He stopped. "And I mean pawn in the most respectful way possible."

Naomi clasped her hands together. "If Protection created me, how can I be a part of Calamity?" She sighed. "But Tal told me I'm a part of Calamity, and he said me knowing that was important."

"So let's consider the impossible," Ferrin offered. "Maybe Protection created you to be like Calamity."

Naomi shook her head. "That wouldn't make sense. Why would Protection create a force just like the one it's fighting against?"

Ferrin frowned. Then he stood. He stared down at her. "Naomi. You've just solved it."

Naomi looked up. "How? I'm still confused."

"You asked why Protection would create something that was equal to Calamity. But the answer is in your question." He reached out and grabbed her hands. "Estell said it this morning. Calamity doesn't have enemies. Its own worst enemy is itself."

Naomi stood. "It has to be defeated by something of equal power." She let go of his hands and gripped the front of his shirt. "So I'm not actually a part of Calamity. I was created to be like it so I can defeat it."

He placed his hands on top of her shoulders. "Yes. It makes sense."

"I just need to solve the quill and pendant puzzle," Naomi said in a rush. "We're so close, Ferrin. We're so close." She smiled, still gripping his chest, but her smile waned.

They were so close to figuring out her purpose. But that meant she was closer to possibly losing Ferrin, too. When this is all over, he may wither away.

"Hey." Ferrin gently lifted her chin with his fingers. He searched her eyes. "Focus on the now."

She swallowed and nodded.

"Now let's go talk with the others," he said quietly. "They'll want to hear what we think."

There was a small rap against the doorframe and Naomi looked up to see Hux.

He cleared his throat. "Sorry to bother, but Vira says we need to leave."

Naomi straightened. "Why?"

"She says she feels something off near the south end of the city." Hux stole a glance at Naomi's arm. "You all good?"

Naomi rubbed the place that Ferrin had healed. "I am now."

Hux lingered, breathing in like he wished to say something more.

"It's okay," Naomi said, reading his mind. "I know you're curious about my blood. But we think Protection created my bloodline for a reason," Naomi reassured. "It was making something of equal power, someone who could defeat The Dark Hand."

Hux cut his eyes to Ferrin.

"It's true," Ferrin agreed. "That's the only thing that makes sense."

Hux blew out a long breath. "So why do we need the quill and pendant?"

"We don't know," Naomi admitted. "But we'll find out. It is all tied together somehow." She strode toward him. "Are we leaving now? Is Vira sure?"

"Vira's sure." Hux looked down at Naomi. "Tell me something. How did you manage to swim all the way back to shore?"

Naomi passed him and grinned over her shoulder. "I just commanded the sea to help me. And it did."

CHAPTER THIRTY-THREE

Tal stood at the double doors of the library building. They were massive and daunting. And they were locked. He stood alone, staring at the shut-up library. Perhaps Deirdre would return soon. She was rarely away, and Tal had an inkling that perhaps even she had some secret business she was attending to. Apparently everyone in Le'Gar had business. And a lot of it had happened under his nose for years. But instead of being angry at himself, he was glad for his own oblivion. Because of it, events had unfolded that could now very well save Thãen.

A breeze ripped through the city, making Tal pull his cloak even tighter. He could wait here for Deirdre, but he didn't want to be recognized by anyone. The King wandering the city alone would surely draw eyes.

He decided to head back to the cathedral and wait, then try the library again. But as he turned to leave, he bumped into the chest of Saul.

"Graves," Tal cursed. "What are you doing here? Hunting for me?"

Saul looked at him with a stoney glare. "Should I be? You

promised a hunt for Naomi Massoud this morning but you have been missing since dawn."

"Your witch didn't wait for my orders," Tal snapped back. "She took it upon herself to search the streets. Thanks to her, Naomi probably realized we were coming."

Saul's mouth sagged. "Have you seen Estell this morning?"

"No. Not since she took off yesterday. You mean she still hasn't returned?"

Saul shook his head and shrugged his massive shoulders. "She must still be out searching."

Tal's stomach tensed. *Or Estell found Naomi.* "Either way, she defied my orders, and I won't work with someone who can't follow my orders in my city."

"She wants to keep the city safe," Saul growled. "Something I thought you would want, too."

King Tal narrowed his eyes. "What are you accusing me of?"

Saul leaned in, his sword clanking at his waist. "You seem divided. Like you're not fully committed to the Dark Hand. You appear to be..." His eyes hardened. "Distant. Secretive."

Tal held his composure. "I am being secretive." He lowered his voice. "We can't let the people of Le'Gar realize we're aiding Calamity."

"Tell me something, "Saul said. "How long have you been a disciple?"

"I was born into it," Tal barked. "I grew up with The Dark Hand. I've always answered to it. Do not question my fealty to Calamity."

"But you lead the city as if you are against it," Saul countered.

Tal sneered. "I have to walk a fine line between my sworn duty to the people and my sworn vow to Calamity." He looked Saul up and down and challenged him. "How did you become a disciple?"

Saul's eyes shifted sideways. "I had nothing to lose and much to gain. When Calamity rules, I won't face death. Neither will you. We'll be spared the slavery. Or whatever else Calamity has planned for Thãen."

"Right." Tal's voice trailed. "Right."

Saul lifted his chin toward the library doors. "So why are you here? What lies inside?"

"Nothing."

He tried to move past Saul, but Saul stepped in front of him.

"I'm not convinced that you're a committed disciple," Saul accused. He narrowed his eyes and pointed to the library door. "Break it down."

Tal shoved him aside. "In case you've forgotten, I'm your king, and *you* take orders from *me*."

"You're not my king," Saul snarled. "That ended when Calamity became my master."

"And you're not my master," Tal growled. "My business here is my own."

Saul drew his sword and aimed it at Tal's chest. "If you're working against Calamity, I will kill you." He cringed, the old Saul peeking out through this new, dark one. "I'm sorry, Tal, but I work solely for The Dark Hand now."

Tal stood still at the point of Saul's sword. "I'm not against Calamity." He scrambled to find a convincing lie. "I came here to destroy something that could help the Massoud."

"All the more reason to break the door down." Saul poked Tal in the chest with the blade. "Do it."

Tal sighed, then he clenched his jaw and said, "You break it down."

Satisfied, Saul faced the door. "Gladly." He lifted his arms above his head and drove the sword into the lock.

Tal glanced over his shoulder, hoping no one was noticing this break-in.

Saul drove his shoulders into the doors. They rattled and gave way. He waved Tal in. "After you, *sir*."

Tal glared. He stepped forward and crossed over the threshold. But before he entered, he cast a thought to the wind.

If someone in Le'Gar has the power to hear me, your assistance is needed here. Come quickly.

CHAPTER THIRTY-FOUR

The morning was crisp, as it usually was in Le'Gar, even in the summer months. In the daylight, Naomi could see that the streets were still a mess from the world's tip. Possessions littered the streets, though people were out with carts, collecting what they could. Dirt coated odd places of the city, like walls and tall columns.

Naomi felt the urgency of the situation as they moved through the havoc. Vira had her cloak hood drawn up over her head as she led Naomi, Ferrin, Hux, and Deirdre through the stone streets. In the early morning hours, Vira had felt a cry for help in the air, so they had all left shortly after that.

Naomi and Deirdre walked side by side, Ferrin ahead of them, behind Vira, while Hux was in the rear. Eli had stayed behind with Millicent. Deirdre reached over and linked Naomi's arm with hers. Namoi could now feel how solid Deirdre was. Naomi had always assumed it was because the librarian was a strong woman, but it was really because she was half bone, half stone.

"Does it hurt?" Naomi asked. "When you shift?"

Deirdre shook her head. "No. I think Protection was kind in giving me powers that don't hurt me."

Naomi nodded, remembering the pain she felt when Estell struck at the roots that she was manipulating. "What special power do you have as part gargoyle?"

"I can communicate with all gargoyles," she revealed, wiping a strand of gray hair out of her eyes. "They'll talk to me because I can become like them. They shouldn't talk to humans, you know."

"Yes, I know," Naomi said, and smiled. It felt like so long ago now that one of the gargoyles, a stone angel, defied its spell and spoke to her, warning her to flee Le'Gar. The angel had crumbled to bits for defying the spell, and Naomi knew then that she had to run away. A gargoyle wouldn't allow itself to be destroyed for no reason. That angel had saved Naomi's life. "I'm thankful every day to the angel who helped me get out of Le'Gar. She spoke to me, even though she knew it would ruin her."

Deirdre nodded, sad, most likely mourning the lost angelic gargoyle.

"So what do you talk to the gargoyles about?" Naomi pressed.

"Well, that's the thing." Deirdre tightened her arm around Naomi's. "I've never felt that my gargoyle state has had much meaning. Of course, maybe Protection had to make me this way so I could have my immortal qualities, but I often think that he didn't have to make me stone to accomplish that."

Naomi gave a small frown. "Maybe your true purpose hasn't been fully discovered."

Deirdre smiled. "That's what I think, too."

The group stopped abruptly when Vira came to a sudden halt.

Naomi looked up as Deirdre dropped her arm. They were in

front of the library. Deirdre's library. And the door was broken in and half hanging on its hinges.

Hux ran to the front of the pack with his sword out. Ferrin followed. They moved shoulder to shoulder up the stone steps with their weapons drawn. Naomi stuck close to Vira as she followed the men close behind.

They crossed the threshold and Naomi held her breath. The library was a disaster. The shelves were empty and all the books were scattered all over the floor. It was difficult to know what had caused the damage—the tip of the world, or a break in.

Deirdre shoved past everyone and ran straight for a spot on the floor. She kicked at it with her heel and Naomi heard a rattle. Like a door in the ground.

"It's still locked," Deirdre said with relief.

"What's down there?" Hux asked.

"Records," she revealed. "Ancestry trees. Secrets. It would be disastrous should anyone find the scrolls down there." Her shoulders sagged. "Many of them were damaged in the first tip."

Vira darted her head around. "Someone's still here. I can feel them."

Ferrin scanned the expansive room. "You're right."

Vira turned to him. "You feel it, too?"

He nodded.

Naomi tried to take in their surroundings quickly, feeling useless since *she* couldn't feel the presence of anyone.

A faint click echoed through the quiet air.

Hux and Ferrin raised their swords in unison.

Naomi tensed. There was another click, like the sound of a boot on the ground.

Then a figure appeared from behind a shelf.

King Tal.

In his hands was a thick sheaf of parchment, unrolled and

large. He stared straight at Naomi, ignoring Hux and Ferrin's swords which were aimed at him.

Ferrin took a step forward. "Raise your hands. Show you're not armed."

Tal obeyed, showing a sword at his hips. The sword had fresh blood on it.

Again, Tal ignored Ferrin and kept his focus on Naomi. "I had to kill him."

Naomi's skin crawled at Tal's intense stare. "Who?"

"Saul," Tal said in a crumbling tone. "He was going to destroy these." He held up the parchment. "I had to make a decision. One that's best for everyone, not just me."

"Where is he?" Vira demanded. "So we know you're being honest."

Tal tilted his head to the left. "Behind the shelf. There."

Together, Hux and Ferrin investigated. With a slow nod of his head, Hux confirmed that Saul's dead body was behind the shelf.

Deirdre pointed to the paper in Tal's hands, apparently familiar. "What blueprints do you have?"

Tal turned the blueprints toward the group. "Raina."

Hux leaned over Tal's shoulder, examining the blueprints to his home city.

Naomi remembered Hux telling her the tale of Raina. How their rivers were red and rumored to be so from ink. "Why do you have Raina's blueprints?" Naomi interrogated Tal. "Last I checked you were a disciple of Calamity."

Tal shook the blueprints, begging her to look. "Please. Don't make me speak about it out loud. I'm on borrowed time. There has been enough death from Calamity in my family." His voice cracked. "Just look here." He shifted Raina's blueprints to reveal another one underneath. Le'Gar's blueprints.

Naomi's heart hurt at the emotion in his voice. *On borrowed time. Death from Calamity?* She knew he spoke of his own death. Then she remembered his father. A recent death in his family. A major one, as his father was the King of Le'Gar, though his father had been sick for quite some time.

"Did your father turn to the Dark Hand?" she asked, keeping her voice low, as if Calamity couldn't hear her. "Is that what happened to him?"

Tal swallowed, tears welling behind his eyes.

His silence was telling.

Deirdre gave a knowing nod. "That would explain why there was no viewing of the body. Something happened to him, didn't it?"

Tal closed his eyes. "He turned on Calamity in his last days. Our family has long been in service to The Dark Hand." He lowered his voice. "But he left me a note. An unfinished one." He nodded toward Naomi. "Until you filled in the blanks for me."

Naomi furrowed her brows. "Me? How?"

"You said the words, Let it flow," Tal said. "In a note warning me, giving me instructions, my father was trying to write that phrase when he died."

"What kind of instructions?" Vira interjected.

"I don't know what they're for," Tal admitted. "But I think I'm starting to understand." He pulled out a piece of paper from his inner jacket. With shaking fingers he unfolded it and began to read. *"Insert the key but warn Le'Gar. Ring the bell. Let—"* He looked up. "Let it flow."

Naomi's heart thudded. "The key. That must mean the quill. We always thought the quill was supposed to write on something, but maybe it needs to be inserted into something like you're saying."

"You have the quill?" Tal asked in disbelief.

Naomi hesitated, but then said, "Yes."

Ferrin drew in a breath, taking a side step toward Naomi in case Tal got any ideas.

But Tal didn't move. He didn't even flinch. "Good."

"What's the bell?" Naomi pressed.

"The bell at the top of the cathedral," Tal informed. "Have you ever heard it before?"

Naomi thought back to all the years she lived in Le'Gar. Never once had she heard it. And it dawned on her why: because the bell was only meant to be used in emergencies. In the event of an immediate evacuation of Le'Gar, the bell would ring in warning.

"The evacuation bell," she said, bright-eyed.

Tal nodded. "Once the quill is inserted into whatever it must be inserted into, the evacuation bell must be rung. But as for why, I don't know." He glanced down at the blueprints. "But I had a strange hunch, and I believe I've figured it out."

Feeling brave, Naomi moved past everyone to be face-to-face with Tal. This close, she could see the flecks of light brown in his eyes mixed with the green. His facial hair had a reddish tint and the lines around his eyes were from frowning, not laughing. Here stood a man who lived life in slavery to a higher power who did not have his best interests in mind, and Naomi truly felt sorry for him.

"What did you figure out?" she asked, eyeing the blueprints.

To her, the blueprints were a jumbled mess of roads and rivers. Building squares and forested borders.

Ferrin waded through the wreckage of books on the floor and found an overturned table. With Hux's help, they righted it.

"Here. Set the prints here," Ferrin ordered Tal.

Tal did as he asked, and soon they were all huddled around it.

Naomi stood wedged between Tal and Ferrin. She followed

Tal's finger as he moved it along squiggly lines running through Raina.

"These are Raina's rivers," Tal informed. He glanced up at Hux. "You would know. You're from there, correct?"

Hux nodded. "I am."

"So you know for a fact that the rivers are red," Tal continued.

Again, Hux confirmed.

"Red rivers aren't normal," Tal stated. "What do the people of Raina say is in the rivers?"

"Ink," Naomi answered for Hux.

Tal raised his eyebrows at her. "Strange? Don't you think?"

"Of course it's strange," Naomi concurred. "But what's the significance of it?"

"The significance begins with Le'Gar's blueprints." Tal shifted Raina's parchment aside and moved Le'Gar's to the front. He dragged his finger over more lines. "Underground tunnels."

Naomi stared at them. "Le'Gar's secret passageways."

"Le'Gar has a lot of them," Tal divulged. "Some are within the city walls, but most of them are underground." He lifted his tired eyes to Ferrin. "You've lived in the city. Long before I ever did. Do you know why the tunnels were created?"

Ferrin seemed at a loss for words, being addressed directly by the King. "No, sir."

"Hm," Tal mumbled, dissatisfied. "It seems nobody knows how they got here or why. But have you ever been inside any of them?"

This time Ferrin said, "Yes." He shifted his weight. "Long ago."

"As have I," Tal disclosed. "And they were wet. How could that be if there is no source of water within them?"

Vira tilted her head. "The Desarian Sea is right there. Could be from sea caves?"

"We have no sea caves," Tal argued with a firm shake of his head.

"So what, then?" Naomi pressed.

"When you line up Raina's blueprints like this…" Tal shifted the blueprints to lie next to Le'Gar like they would appear if they were on a world map. "The rivers all run in this direction." He moved his finger along the rivers again. "And when they end, they connect perfectly with the blueprints of our underground tunnels."

Naomi watched as Tal's finger left Raina's blueprints and slid directly onto Le'Gar's where the underground passages were. And he was right. They lined up. It looked as if Raina's rivers could flow right into Le'Gar's tunnels.

"Let it flow," Naomi whispered. "Let Raina's rivers flow into Le'Gar's tunnels?"

Tal smiled up at her. Soft and sorry. "Perhaps."

Hux crossed one arm over his chest and frowned. "But how is Raina's river water supposed to get here? If they were connected to the tunnels here, wouldn't the tunnels already be flooded?"

"I don't know," Tal admitted.

They stood in silence. A golden witch, a Magnificent, a human gargoyle, a treasonist, a king, and a girl made by and from a god. Together they were a force to be reckoned with, but lack of knowledge was enough to stop them. So close, yet so far. And Naomi could hardly take it.

"We can't give up," she said with a bite. She looked at Tal. "What else? What else can you tell me?"

"Nothing," he admitted softly. "I've given you everything I can."

She turned to Ferrin. "Come on. Try to feel something." She

begged with her eyes. "Please. Can't you feel a pull in any direction? You're a Magnificent." When he didn't answer fast enough, she spun to Vira. "Vira? Anything?"

"I can't just summon a feeling, Naomi," she said gently. "I'm sorry."

Naomi gripped Ferrin's shirt sleeve and bore into his eyes. "Come *on*. You can do everything. *Search*."

"Naomi." He removed her grip from his arm and held onto her hands gently. "I can't do everything. I have limits. I'm not a god."

She drew away from him in frustration. They couldn't stop now. There was no time. They were running out of time. Thãen was going to fall. Months or weeks, but Naomi felt in her heart that the final tip was only days away.

Closing her eyes, she said a prayer. *Please help us, Protection. Please help us, Mavelic.*

Her eyes flung open as the whole ground jolted.

Ferrin reached for her and she reached for him as the floor slanted slightly. Their hands collided and Naomi held on tight.

Hux braced himself against a shelf and Vira clung to his side. Tal slipped, but managed to cling to the same shelf.

Books slid across the floor, sliding down with the floor's angle.

Deirdre jolted and her body rippled and thunked to stone. Her stone angel form took over, and she held her wings up as a shield as more books and parts of the ceiling fell like hail. Her wingspan was nearly eight feet wide, and with every piece of debris she endured, she stood sturdy.

Naomi ducked at the pieces of plaster that missed Deirdre's wings, but she never took her eyes off of her. In this form, Deirdre was immaculate. An unbeatable force. But Naomi straightened when she saw Deirdre's right wing.

Each wing was made of gray stone, but feathers were intricately etched into them. So detailed that each individual one was noticeable. And that's how Naomi noticed a gaping spot on Deirdre's right wing. A spot where a feather should be but was not. A spot that was the same size as the quill.

"Deirdre!" Naomi shouted.

The ground tipped again, this time the other way. Ferrin nearly lost his footing, but Naomi held him up with her entire body.

There was a thunderous jolt and the ground thudded back into place. The world was upright again.

Naomi shoved her hands beneath Ferrin's shirt and grabbed the quill that sat against his body.

"What are you doing?" he asked, alarmed.

Deirdre lowered her wings and began to draw them into her body. But Naomi left the safety of Ferrin's side and dove toward the stone angel. She held the quill up for Deirdre to see.

"It's you," Naomi said, breathless. "You're the lock."

Deirdre's solid eyes bore into Naomi. She stood still, her wings still partially outstretched.

Naomi took a step forward and lifted the quill toward her right wing.

Slowly, Deirdre lowered her wing to Naomi's level.

With trembling hands, Naomi touched the tip of the golden quill to the pendant of her necklace. The quill filled with light.

Then she took the shining quill and slid it into the space on Deirdre's wing.

CHAPTER THIRTY-FIVE

Light erupted from the quill. Like the flow of molasses, the glow began to spread over Deirdre's entire body. In a matter of seconds, the stone angel was solid gold and shining like the sun.

Naomi stepped back, wanting to shield her eyes but not daring to look away. She backed into Ferrin who pulled her slightly back as Deirdre began to speak.

Her mouth opened and a voice that was not her own came out. It was deep and hollow. All-consuming and boisterous. It struck Naomi to the core, and she knew she was standing in the presence of the power of Protection.

"The time is now for the plan to come forth." Deirdre's lips said, and Naomi clung to every word. *"An heir from the Massoud seed must use nature as a weapon to draw Calamity into the city of Le'Gar and trap it. Release the rivers of Raina and let them flow into the tunnels of Le'Gar. The red rivers will flood the whole city, but it must be done. The ink in the waters will blot out Calamity, covering its existence, drowning it for good. Calamity will put up a fight. It will try to escape. But the gargoyles know what to do. They will create a barrier around and above the city. They will hold The Dark Hand*

captive until it is drowned." Deirdre's head slowly rotated to face Naomi. *"The time is now, Massoud."*

Then Deirdre's light blinked out. She was gray again. And she collapsed to the floor.

Naomi rushed forward and held her as her stone self retracted and somehow melted back to her human form. She was once again the librarian Naomi had come to know. She blinked, staring up at Naomi.

"Are you alright?" Naomi asked, cradling her.

Deirdre sat upright and felt around the ground. "The quill is gone."

Naomi touched Deirdre's shoulder. "I don't think we need it anymore. We've been told the instructions. Now all we have to do is act."

Hux paced, wiping at his mouth in a nervous tick.

Vira watched him from the corner of her eyes. "What is it?"

"I think I have to go," he said softly.

Ferrin nodded slowly.

Tal curled both hands into fists and breathed out one long, calm breath. "I have to ring the bell. We need to evacuate the city."

Naomi closed her eyes. "One thing at a time." She looked over at Hux. "Why do you have to leave?"

"I have to go to Raina," he said, matter of fact. "I know Raina the best out of all of us. I can figure out how to release the rivers."

"And I think you'll have help," Ferrin pointed out. "Maya is more willing to help than you think."

Hux gave a single nod. "It's confirmed then. I'll go and release the rivers."

"Hux, wait—" Vira tried.

But Tal cut her off. "How long will it take for you to get to Raina?"

"Two days," he answered quickly.

"If you don't run into trouble," Naomi countered.

"But at least two," Tal confirmed.

Hux nodded again.

"That gives the people of Le'Gar at least two days to get out and head into the mountains where there is higher ground," Tal said with relief. "It's not a lot of time, but it's better than a few hours."

"I'll leave now," Hux said. "Do you have a horse I can use?"

"I do," Tal said. "We'll get you one immediately."

Everything suddenly started to move terribly fast. Hux and Tal charged for the library door. Naomi helped Deirdre to her feet and watched as Ferrin followed Hux to the exit.

"I'll head for the cathedral to ring the bell," Tal called over his shoulder. "The more time our people have to get out, the better."

"Agreed," Ferrin said in a monotone.

Naomi swallowed, hanging back as everyone began to rush. Things were happening. The tides were turning. Ferrin's time here was dwindling.

"I'm not ready," Naomi whispered to herself.

But Vira heard her.

"You must be ready," Vira said, her voice shaky. "We must all be ready."

Naomi fought back tears as Vira joined her at her side. Vira's presence had always been overpowering in the best way possible, but right now, even her aura was stale. Hesitant. Sad.

"Do you know something I don't?" Naomi asked with dread.

Vira's mouth turned down. "What do you mean?"

Naomi faced her. "You're scared."

Vira shook her head. "I'm not afraid of what's to come, Omi, but it does weigh heavy on my heart that I'm in the unknown."

Naomi rocked back, understanding. As a golden witch, Vira

had a sixth sense. A knowing. Visions and feelings. But right now, she had nothing. She was empty. They only had the words of Protection spoken through Deirdre to go on.

"This is what we've been trying to accomplish," Naomi said, in an attempt to comfort Vira, but she was also trying to comfort herself.

"It is," Vira agreed, "but we don't have to pretend we aren't afraid. Fear doesn't make us incapable of action, it just makes us human." She smiled. "Because though I'm a golden witch, I'm still human."

Ferrin turned at the library door toward Namoi, Vira, and Deirdre. Hux and Tal had already left.

"Is something wrong?" he asked with genuine concern.

Naomi shook her head. "No. We're just discussing details."

"Yes, details," Vira said matter-of-fact. "We can't act in haste. We must have a plan."

"We do have a plan," Ferrin countered. "Hux is going to Raina. Tal is ringing the bell. The evacuation is going to start."

"But how am I supposed to summon Calamity to Le'Gar?" Naomi inquired. "We can't release the rivers in Raina if we don't have Calamity trapped here."

Deirdre, who had been oddly silent, pointed to the broken library doors that were open, moving from an oncoming wind. "A storm is coming."

Naomi and Ferrin locked eyes.

"You can command the sea," he said in a hush. "I think you can command a storm."

"High winds," Vira pointed out. "Could you use the storm to draw Calamity in?"

Naomi balled her fists at her side. "I can try."

"You have to do more than try," Deirdre said firmly. "You have to succeed. We only have one shot." She closed her eyes.

"And the gargoyles are stirring. I can feel it. They haven't been released yet, but they know their time is coming."

Naomi stared out the door into the gray streets, darkening as if the wind itself was black. "Who has to release the gargoyles?"

Ferrin tilted his head. "Naomi, I think it's you."

Naomi pointed to herself. "Me? How?"

"I'm not sure," he admitted, "but you've been the key to everything so far."

"What about Deirdre?" Naomi asked, jerking an elbow in her direction.

"No," Deirdre said quickly. "It's not me. I'm done." She shook her arms out. "I feel heavy. I feel...like stone."

Naomi touched Deirdre's hand, to feel the softness of her skin, but to her surprise it *wasn't* soft. It was rough. Like a rock.

Deirdre faced them. "I'll be leaving you soon. My purpose is over."

Ferrin cleared his throat. "We need to get going. Tal is on his way to fetch a horse for Hux. Hux will be leaving soon."

At the mention of Hux, Vira stiffened. "Where is he now?"

"Heading to Eli's," Ferrin said. Then his lips tightened. "What about Millie, Vira? She'll need to evacuate."

Vira squeezed her eyes shut. "I know."

Naomi faced Vira with a stern set of eyes. "Go with her, Vira."

When Vira opened her eyes, they were misty. "Go with her? Naomi, you don't know what you're asking of me. You're asking me to abandon you to do this task all alone."

Naomi grabbed both of Vira's hands. "I was never alone. You got me this far. You did your job. You found me and you helped me. Now go be with your daughter. Keep her safe. Keep yourself safe."

Vira dropped Naomi's hands and pulled her into a hug. Something they had never done before.

Blinking back tears Naomi whispered, "I'll find you when this is all over."

"You must," Vira ordered.

When they withdrew, Naomi glanced over at Ferrin. "Are you ready, ranger?"

He smiled then. "I am, Ms. Smyth."

CHAPTER THIRTY-SIX

L e'Gar was laden in black. Clouds suffocated the sky, the color of charcoal. The wind roared. But the rain held off. For now.

Eli's home was lit with warm lamp light. Everyone was in the living space, not wanting to be apart. Excitement and anticipation surged through the air. They were days away from stealing back their world from the grip of Calamity. Should they succeed, Calamity would be destroyed forever. A life with Protection was ahead. A life of light. A light the world hasn't seen for centuries.

Hux fastened his sword at his hip and adjusted a bag against his back. His boots were laced. His shirt buttoned to his neck. He was ready to go.

Eli peeked out the front window. "Tal's coming up the way with your horse now."

Wind blew down the chimney and into the room through the fireplace. The chill struck Naomi and she shivered, thinking of Estell. Estell who disappeared but wasn't gone. She was still out there somewhere.

Millicent stuck close to Vira's side. Vira kissed her on top of the head then stepped toward Hux. She brushed her hands over the tops of his shoulders, as if smoothing him out. "Ride fast. And be safe."

Hux's cheeks twitched, but he remained still. "I will. And I'll see you when this is all over." He smiled. "When there is nothing but light again."

Vira's face quivered. "I've thought about everything you've ever said about us."

Hux frowned. "And?"

"And I think we missed our chance," she admitted, breathless. "But maybe when this is all over, we can start again. Start something new."

He smiled, his eyes crinkling. "Okay. It's a deal."

Vira stepped back as a knock came from Eli's door.

Eli opened it to reveal Tal standing there with a horse at the end of a rope. Wind whipped his cloak around and he had to shout over the sound. "Time to go! Storm's tearing in from the Desarian Sea!"

Ferrin gave Hux a firm handshake. "Be safe."

Hux nodded. "And you."

Hux kissed Millicent on the head, gave Deirdre a hug, then he stopped at Naomi right before the door.

She looked up at him, her eyelashes fluttering, trying to hold back tears. But she felt confident in Hux. She knew he was more than an everyday Rider. He was a hero. A force. Someone who would give all he had before he gave up.

"You can change the times," he spoke to her, strong and definite. "*You*. You, who are both human and god. You, who are humble and afraid. You, who are capable and strong."

"I'm going to do it," she shouted over the wind. "But I never could have done any of it without you."

He pulled her into a hug and she made it a point to remember the feeling. His hair against her cheek. Her fingertips pressed into his back. The way his arm cradled the back of her head.

Then he pulled away, gave everyone one last glance, and stepped out the door. Tal handed him the reins and Hux hoisted himself onto the horse's back. With a pull of the reins, the horse turned around and bolted up the empty, treacherously windy, dark-as-night street. Hux's large form sat hunched forward, leaning into the wind. Then he looped around the corner and disappeared from view.

Tal stood in the doorframe, the wind tearing at his back.

Naomi locked eyes with him. "It's time to ring the bell."

CHAPTER THIRTY-SEVEN

Rain began to fall in big drops. They were cold and splotchy against Tal's skin as he ran through the streets. Streets absent of people but still littered with items from the world's tips.

He had never seen such black clouds before. This wasn't a normal storm. This was something else. Something conjured up by the forces of the Outer Void. The wind was loud, like the roar of a wave.

It took everything in him to keep running against the weather. His feet pounded into the ground and he breathed heavily. The cathedral came into view and his eyes drifted upward to the bell tower. The bell sat still, a goblin gargoyle perched on the outer wall of the belfry. To access the belfry, he had to climb hundreds of wooden stairs within the walls of the tower.

But his chest hurt. Fatigue nearly brought him to his knees. Either the weather was beating his defeated body to its core, or something else was affecting him.

Even so, he kept running. He must ring the bell. Hux was already on the way to Raina. If the plan worked out, the rivers would flood the entire city of Le'Gar. His people had to evacuate.

He was almost to the cathedral when a pain so piercing and lightning-like struck his chest. He cried out and fell to his knees.

Another pain, equally as intense, sent him sprawling. He clutched at his chest and whimpered, feeling the air leaving his lungs.

The rain suddenly started to fall in slow motion around him. He blinked, peering up at the rooftops of Le'Gar. The peeks towered into the sky, as if they were spearing the black clouds. But between the clouds he saw light. A light so bright it made him smile.

He closed his eyes but opened them a moment later, choosing to look one last time. The griffin at the top of the cathedral looked down at him. It nodded at him through the gray rain.

But Calamity had won. Tal had proved to be disloyal, therefore Calamity had made its move to take his life.

Then Tal took one last breath and wrapped his arms around himself. He had done everything he could.

With a final exhale, Tal succumbed to death.

The cathedral bell remained silent in his passing.

He was a king who was too late, but a king who saw light at the end.

CHAPTER THIRTY-EIGHT

Ferrin paced in front of Eli's fireplace.

Naomi watched him from the couch, gnawing on her fingernails.

"Why haven't we heard the bell yet?" Ferrin asked, running a hand through his hair.

Naomi shrugged, trying to hide her anxieties. "Maybe something stopped him."

"Like Estell," Ferrin grumbled.

Naomi hugged her core. She had the same thought. Surely Estell hadn't abandoned her duties of stopping them at all costs. Estell was practically an equal with Calamity at this point. An equal threat, at least.

Vira continued to package food in brown paper sacks in the kitchen. Naomi could hear rustling and low murmuring as Vira spoke to her daughter.

"You don't think it was wrong of me to tell Vira to evacuate with everyone else, do you?" she asked Ferrin.

Ferrin shook his head. "No. Millicent needs her mother." He sort of smiled. "And you have me. I'm going to stay with you every second."

Naomi nodded. "Where should I go to summon the storm?"

"The cliff along the pines," he answered quickly. "It gives you the perfect view of the entirety of Le'Gar. You'll have the sea below you and the mountains at your back. Nature will surround you."

Again she nodded, but she was unsure. Of herself. Of the plan.

"What if it doesn't work?" she whispered.

Ferrin stopped pacing and faced her. "When will you believe in yourself?"

She closed her eyes. "When this is over."

A shadow stretched across the floor as Eli entered the room and stood just beside the fire. His eyes looked older. His skin more wrinkled. And when he looked at Ferrin, worry sat as a mask over his entire face.

Ferrin snapped his head toward him. "What's happened?"

Naomi rose, twisting her fingers.

Eli shook his head. "Tal didn't make it."

"He was intercepted?" Naomi guessed.

"No," Eli lamented. "Calamity took him. I saw Tal in a vision. He's passed away."

Naomi held a hand over her mouth. Their poor king. Their poor, confused, manipulated, king.

But now there was a worse problem. No one had rung the cathedral bell. Le'Gar's people were still oblivious to the fact that a flood was coming.

Vira drifted into the living room, hearing the commotion. "Tal's dead?"

"I'm afraid so," Eli confirmed. "And now it's up to us to finish what he couldn't."

Vira's voice was soft, desperate. "Please let me help."

But Millicent crept up behind Vira, holding a bag. Ready to go. Prepared to flee.

"You can't stay," Ferrin said with force. He motioned to Millicent. "Now your purpose is her."

Millicent stood taller. "Mum, if you need to leave again, that's okay. Deirdre can take me out of the city."

Vira closed her eyes and blinked away oncoming tears. "No, love. You and I will be leaving together. Because Ferrin's right." She turned and stroked her daughter's hair. "You and I have been apart for too long. I will not leave you again."

Millicent smiled up at her mom. She didn't say anything, but she didn't have to. Her smile spoke for itself. *Thanks for choosing me.*

Naomi felt a wave of peace, knowing that sending Vira on her way was the right and only thing to do. But that meant their journey together ended here.

Because Naomi was going to ring the bell.

"Ferrin," Naomi spoke, sharp. She locked eyes with him. "Let's get to the bell."

Eli clasped a hand on Ferrin's shoulder. "Go."

"Will you be leaving with everyone else?" Ferrin asked, sorrow slipping into his tone.

Eli chortled. "You think I'd let you do this alone now? No, I'll not be leaving. Not yet, anyway. I'll be here, waiting for Calamity's arrival." He turned to Naomi. "And should it give you trouble, I'll be here to offer whatever power I can, as I know Ferrin will do, too."

Naomi swallowed, wanting to cry. To feel not only supported but protected was something she hadn't had since she lost her father. It wasn't until Ferrin found her, running away from Le'Gar all those months ago, that she didn't feel alone. And now, she had the full commitment of two Magnificents. Both of which cared for her. One more so than the other, but both were committed to her nonetheless.

"I owe you all my life," she choked.

"I wouldn't speak about giving your life before a battle with the gods," Eli teased with light in his aging eyes.

Naomi smiled and gave a miniscule laugh. "I suppose you're right."

Vira sniffed, then rolled her shoulders back, standing tall. "I'll be waiting in the mountains for you." Her voice wavered. "This is not goodbye, but a 'see you when the darkness has gone'."

Naomi reached out and took Vira's hands. The hands that braided her hair in Zul when they first met. The hands that belonged to the woman who took an arrow for her sake.

"And what a bright day that will be," Naomi said, her voice plugged up with emotion. "I'll see you on the other side."

CHAPTER THIRTY-NINE

Naomi and Ferrin ran side by side through Le'Gar. The rain pelted them, leaving behind spots that stung. The roar of the Desarian Sea echoed through the rocky crevices of the city. Every door was shut tight. Every window sealed against the wild storm. The people knew something ominous was happening, but they didn't yet know that staying here was the wrong decision.

As she ran, Naomi looked up. A flash of lightning illuminated the enveloping clouds and silhouetted the gargoyles. Their horns struck the sky like thorns. Their wings stretched out as if to take off. But still, none of them left their post. They were still frozen in place.

The cathedral was dead ahead now. Ferrin picked up speed, and Naomi kept up. She didn't even stop when they charged past Tal's soggy, lifeless body in the street. She simply kept her eyes forward, not daring to lament over the loss of their king.

Ferrin sprinted up the cathedral's stone steps and threw his hand out, casting a wave of energy at the doors. They both slammed open, revealing startled guards who lifted their swords at once.

"We're here on the King's business," Ferrin tried, panting.

But the guards didn't back down.

With a defeated grunt Ferrin sent another wave of energy rolling through the air. It hit the guards and sent them tumbling backward. It gave him and Naomi just enough of a chance to dart down the side hallway to the arched wooden door leading to the stairs of the belfry.

Naomi stayed right on Ferrin's heels as he took the stairs two at a time. She could hear the distant shouting of the guards in the entry hall below and it gave her the motivation to keep charging upward. Stair after stair, turn after turn, until her legs ached and burned. But the bell was closer now than ever. Even now, she could feel wet air, telling her they were nearing the top where the bell hung behind four stone half-walls.

The stairs ended at a wooden ladder and Ferrin climbed it. Naomi sucked in a breath and followed him up. Her head broke through an open square hole and wind and rain whipped her hair around. Ferrin reached down and tugged her to her feet.

Ferrin had to shout over the wind. "The rope for the bell is over there!" He pointed past the brass bell that was so large it could crush a small building if it were to fall.

The belfry was a square. Four half walls and a roof over the bell were the only shield against the weather. And it was hardly enough. The rain hit Naomi in the eyes as she strained to see the rope hanging near the bell on the other side of the tower. All she had to do was run. In a few long strides she would be there. In seconds the city would know that danger is approaching.

Naomi shoved past Ferrin, even as he himself made for the bell's rope.

One, two, three steps. She was almost there.

But a swarm of black smoke, hissing with the wind, rushed into the belfry with wicked speed. It curled around Naomi, cutting off her breath, and chilling her from skin to bone. She skidded to a stop, slipping on the slick stone, as the black vapor materialized in front of her.

The black dissipated and golden skin and silvery white hair took its place. Estell stood there, her slender body fully clothed in black feathers. Her eyes were yellow like a hawk's. Her fingernails thin and pointed like claws.

Naomi struggled to breathe at the sight of the golden witch. She was no longer of this world. She was half human, half morbid god. A creature of bad decisions.

As soon as Estell took form, Ferrin threw a wave of energy at her. The invisible force slammed into her, but it rebounded, hitting Naomi instead.

Naomi rocketed backward and crashed into the half wall behind her. She hit the wall hard and felt the stone scrape the back of her head as she slumped to her side.

Estell cackled and snapped her fingers. A black flame appeared between her thumb and forefinger. She blew on the flame and it grew into a large, flaming ball. She sent it sailing toward Naomi.

Ferrin threw himself in front of Naomi, standing wide and pushing out his chest. He squeezed his eyes shut as the flame hit a thin wall of energy between him and the flame. It was enough to save his own skin and the black flame hissed as it tumbled sideways and sailed over the half wall into the rain.

Naomi struggled to sit up. Her eyes were blurry. Her body still cold from Estell's presence.

Ferrin placed a hand on Naomi's shoulder, forcing her to stay down. He kept his back to her and used his entire body to block her from Estell.

Naomi tried to fight against him. She needed to stand. She needed to fight! But Ferrin kept her down, digging his fingers into her collarbone.

"I'm going to kill her, Fer-rin," Estell taunted, drawing out his name, as if the name itself was something to savor.

"You've tried so many times," he shot back. "Yet she lives."

Her eyes gleamed with fury. "Because of you."

Ferrin laughed. A maniac sound. "You think I'll back down now?"

"You have no choice," Estell sneered. "Because I'll kill you first."

The golden witch screamed then, a swarm of flies rushing from her mouth. They swarmed Ferrin, and he let go of Naomi. He threw both arms up, casting energy that pulsed the flies away into the storm, but Estell was already on him.

She slammed into him and pinned him to the soaking ground. Both of his wrists were in each of her hands. She straddled him, forcing him down even though he writhed beneath her.

Naomi dragged herself to her hands and knees, her vision still foggy and spinning from her collision with the wall. But seeing Ferrin trapped beneath the woman who ruined his life was enough to get her moving. She moved toward him, knees scraping stone. The storm raged around the belfry, whipping her soaked hair around her eyes. She squeezed her eyes shut and tried to take control of the storm. Little fragments of the wind slid into her grasp and she tried to throw them at Estell, but she kept losing control. Her fatigue and panic clouded her mind, making her weak and uncontrolled.

Estell saw Naomi coming and snickered, then as a flash of lightning illuminated the bell, the golden witch raised both clawed hands and sank them into Ferrin's chest.

CHAPTER FORTY

"No!" Naomi screamed.

The world seemed to slow. The wind and rain went mute in her ears. All that was clear was Estell, her fingers stuck in Ferrin's chest. And even though Naomi wanted to rip her eyes away from the shock on Ferrin's face, she couldn't bring herself to do it. She couldn't abandon him while he was in pain. While there were claws buried inside of him.

"Ferrin!" she cried over the storm.

When she wailed his name, he blinked and looked at her. The browns and greens of his eyes swam with watery tears. Tears of physical pain. Naomi wanted to cry herself, but something else took over inside of her. Anger.

She rose to her knees and screamed. With her mouth wide open, she hurled the emotion at Estell in ear piercing rage. Her body shook. Her fists were clenched so tightly that her fingernails broke the skin of her palms.

Estell yanked her claws out of Ferrin's body and covered her ears.

Naomi kept screaming.

The bell rattled as the entire belfry began to vibrate.

Naomi felt the sudden movement, but she wasn't finished yet. She wouldn't stop screaming until her anger was expelled. She wouldn't let one drop remain in her system. She would let Estell know just how much she loved Ferrin. Not because she had to, but because she had no choice. Her anger would have to bleed out, otherwise it would kill her.

So she out-voiced the storm. Her cry rose above the lashing wind and pounding rain. Even the thunder was quiet compared to her. The louder she hollered, the harder the belfry shook.

And the fear on Estell's face deepened.

The golden witch still had her palms against her ears, staring at Naomi in utter astonishment. She slunk off of Ferrin, cowering as if she were in pain.

The bell swayed. The tower groaned.

Then the sound of cracking reverberated around the belfry. Estell cried out.

Naomi wavered for a moment when she saw what was happening to Estell's body. Each black feather surrounding the golden witch was bending and breaking. Like a finger being snapped.

"Stop!" Estell wailed. "Stop!"

Even if Naomi wanted to stop, she couldn't. Her screams turned into a cry as she focused on the holes in Ferrin's chest. His breathing was shallow, but his eyes were still open. She dragged herself to him.

Estell grappled for Naomi, but when she made contact with Naomi's arm, her claws retracted.

Then Estell's fingers began to fade, turning translucent. Like a ghost.

"You're destroying me," Estell whispered, the fight gone from her voice.

Naomi sat back on her heels, soaking wet, terribly cold, and exhausted. Her throat was raw. Her screaming had finally stopped. Ferrin lay in front of her and Estell sat on the other side of him, her body turning to fog.

"I have power over you," Naomi rasped. "You may serve The Dark Hand, but I don't. I'm its worst enemy."

Estell looked down at her body. She was fully ghost-like now. "Calamity will save me."

For the first time, Naomi felt true sadness for Estell. "No. It used you, and now you're useless to it." She sucked in a breath. "I'm sorry."

"If you're truly sorry, reverse it!" Estell screamed. "Reverse it! I surrender to you! I surrender to you, Naomi Massoud, please save me."

Naomi's lips quivered. "I don't know how. It's too late."

Estell went still. Her body flickered. "Where will I go?" She sounded afraid.

Naomi shook her head. "I don't know. And I don't care." She swallowed. "As long as your darkness is gone."

Then Naomi inhaled, her emotions tucked away, and she caught the power of the wind. *Take her away.*

A monstrous gust swept into the belfry and twirled around Estell. A moment later the ghost of Estell was caught up in the spinning air. And the golden witch didn't so much as whimper when the wind swept her out into the storm, carrying the mist that had once been her somewhere far, far away from Thãen.

With tears flooding her eyes, Naomi rose to shaky legs and stepped over Ferrin, forcing herself to ignore him when his hand faintly reached up to touch her. She trudged her way over to the bell's rope and wrapped trembling hands around it. With every ounce of strength she had left, she gave a powerful tug. The wheel supporting the rope groaned and the bell rocked back and forth, slow and silent at first, but then a long, bellowing gong rang out. Naomi kept pulling, hearing the foreboding tune of the bell echoing through the city.

She let go of the rope and stood there, staring out at the rooftops of Le'Gar. Something inside of her burned. A fire in her chest.

Against her will, she opened her mouth and began to speak. "Gargoyles of Le'Gar, you are released in the name of Mavelic."

Le'Gar began to shake. The sound of stone ripping away from stone thundered through the storm. Shadows took to the sky. The cries of griffins and goblins echoed against the city walls. Through walls of rain, Naomi could see the thousands of gargoyles breaking free from their permanent places. The gargoyles with wings soared through the air, others crawled down the buildings to the streets. They were like an army of stone ants gathering to protect their home.

Then a hand gripped Naomi's wrist.

She flung around, drawing her sword, but it clattered to the ground when she came face-to-face with a dripping wet, very much alive Ferrin.

"Graves!" she cried, and flung herself on him. She wrapped her arms so tightly around his neck that she feared she may suffocate him, but she wanted nothing more than for her chest to be pressed up against his. She wanted to feel him breathing. To know this was real.

Ferrin held her just as tight, and that's when Naomi felt just how solid Ferrin's chest was. Unnaturally solid.

She drew back and placed both hands over the holes still present in his chest. But what sat beneath her fingers was rigid and cold, and for the first time she realized that there was no blood.

Without removing Naomi's hands, Ferrin unbuttoned his

shirt. He peeled away the fabric to reveal a metal chest plate. One with a tusked elephant engraved upon the front.

"Hux's chest plate," Naomi whispered.

The metal had punctures in it from Estell's claws, but when Ferrin lifted it off over his head, his bare skin had miniscule gashes. Superficial. Non-life-threatening.

"Hux gave it to me before he left," Ferrin said. "I had a dream the other night. One that I told Hux about. In the dream I was gasping for breath and clutching my chest." He rubbed a slow hand over the marks on his skin. "Now I know it was a prophecy. And I know that Hux has saved my life."

Naomi placed shaking hands on his wounds. His skin was warm, matching the feeling in her stomach. "Thank Protection that he did."

Ferrin held her hands against his chest. "And you saved Le'Gar."

"Not yet."

Ferrin nudged his chin toward the rain outside the belfry. "Take a look, Omi."

Naomi's back was to the city, and when she turned, pride rose from her chest to her throat. The city, once closed up and hibernating from the storm, had come to life. Groups of people huddled together and ran through the streets toward the mountains. Lanterns were lit inside dark buildings. Shouts rang into the air from the east side of the city to the west. The people were evacuating.

But the gargoyles weren't fleeing. They were preparing to stay and fight.

Once bound to one place, perched over Le'Gar, the gargoyles now gathered and crawled through the city. Most headed to the outskirts to form a barrier. A fence to keep in The Dark Hand. The gargoyles with wings soared in swarms above Le'Gar's peaks, like a painting of angels on a cathedral ceiling. The rest roamed the streets like hungry lions, pacing, searching, as if patrolling. Perhaps searching for Naomi to protect.

Yes, Naomi had released the gargoyles. Now the fate of Le'Gar wasn't just in her hands, but also in the wings of the beasts of stone.

She turned back to Ferrin, and he placed a gentle hand on the side of her face.

"How did you destroy Estell?" he said in a hush.

Naomi blinked, watching his mouth move, savoring his touch. "I screamed."

One side of his mouth twitched upward. "Well, I know that. But how did that end her? How did your screams have such power over everything that she was?"

"I don't think Estell's darkness could handle the light. I screamed out of anger because I thought I lost someone I loved. I loved too hard, and she hated too much. In the end, when we clashed, I won. Light is the true power, because it chases away the shadows. Darkness will always be forced to flee when faced with light."

Ferrin kissed her forehead and left his lips there. "You've always been a light. Especially for me."

She leaned into his lips. "Is it time to bring the light back to Thãen?"

"Not yet," he said, pulling away. "Hux has only been gone for a few hours. We need to at least give him the two days he needs. If you draw Calamity to Le'Gar before Hux is able to release the rivers, then you'll have to hold The Dark Hand here for a long time, and you may not be able to do that. Not to mention the people here need more time to leave."

Naomi's insides churned. "What about the people here who can't move well? The elderly and injured?"

Ferrin nodded, looking out at the city below. "We have time

yet before we provoke Calamity. Let's spend it making sure we see that everyone gets out."

"If the storm stops before it's time to capture Calamity, I won't have the wind to use to my advantage."

"I wouldn't worry about that. Protection sent this storm. If The Hand of Protection meant for you to use the wind and rain, it will sustain the weather until you're ready to control it."

CHAPTER FORTY-ONE

Hux's thighs burned from clinging so tightly to his horse for two days. He had only slept for six hours in the last forty-eight, and the only thing keeping him alert was pure adrenaline. The mountain had been quiet and blessedly dry for most of the journey. But the silence sometimes suffocated him. For months he had eaten, slumbered, walked, ran, and fought with people whom he would now consider family. Being alone never scared him before. And it didn't scare him now. But it did leave him empty. Especially when he neared the city of Raina and he noticed smoke rising up from the trees in the distance. Something wasn't right in the city, and as he urged his horse to trot faster, he dreaded facing whatever lay ahead, alone.

Raina was similar to Le'Gar in that it was surrounded by a high stone wall. And usually Raina had guards placed around the city, also just like Le'Gar. But as Hux rode up, there were no guards present. He halted his horse for only a second as he stared up at the wall. There was no question as to why the guards were gone: parts of the city were ablaze and shouting reverberated within its walls. The guards were needed inside.

Hux drove his heels into his horse's side and galloped in through the city's main entrance. Into chaos.

Raina's streets were littered with debris from Thãen's tip, just like Le'Gar. Standing within the debris, flooding the streets, were Raina's people. They shouted. Screamed. They threw torches at buildings. What usually was Raina's street market was on fire. And the angry people kept chanting the same thing in a harsh cadence:

De-throne the King! De-throne the King!

Hux pulled his horse to a halt, not having much space to weave his way through the sea of furious rioters. He darted his eyes in every direction, trying to pinpoint a route he could take to get to King Leeland's royal fortress. Yes, he knew that appearing before Leeland face-to-face meant facing the man he committed treason against, but he would have to risk it. If Leeland really did want to defeat Calamity, he would listen to Hux and help him figure out how to release the rivers. Or maybe Leeland already knew. Either way, Hux needed his help.

He tugged his horse sideways and forced his way into the crowd.

The rioters hardly parted for him. In fact, some only paid him mind just to curse at him.

"Who are *you*?" a teenage boy spat. "A Rider? You're as corrupt as the King!"

That got the whole group surrounding Hux fired up. They looked at him and his horse and spewed death threats. They blamed him for being loyal to the King. Someone threw a brick at him and he deflected it just in time with his limp arm. He cringed, gritting his teeth at the pain, and leaned forward to urge his horse faster.

"He's the treasonist!" a woman cried from the crowd. "Look at his arm. Look at him!"

"The treasonist is back!" someone hollered joyfully. "He's come to dethrone the King!"

"No," Hux tried to deflect their comments. "No, I've come to negotiate with him."

A woman grabbed his thigh. "Don't let the King persuade you into supporting his plan. He wants to provoke the gods! He wants war!"

Hux pulled his leg away and forced his horse forward. He might as well have been trudging through quicksand. No matter how urgently he tried to move, the people slowed him down. He was getting nowhere. He was a stick in the mud.

But up ahead a group of Riders stood in a line. Their horses were shoulder to shoulder and they seemed to be blocking off a street. The street that led to the King's fortress.

Hux gently kicked his horse and forced his way over to the Riders. Rioters screamed at them, threw heavy items, books, bricks, rocks. The rioters were relentless, and Hux's chest tightened at the thought that perhaps King Leeland had deteriorated because of his obsession to defeat The Dark Hand. That maybe when the quill was thought to be lost again, King Leeland sought another plan of action and was acting impulsively instead of being thorough and thinking clearly. A sliver of regret passed through Hux's veins. He had committed treason, but for good reason. He just had to remind himself of that. If he had retrieved the quill and brought it to King Leeland, Naomi would have never gained possession of it. And perhaps Leeland would have done something reckless. It seemed, from the rioters, that the King *was* acting reckless.

Hux raised an arm to grab the attention of the Riders in front of him. Their expressions flashed from grim to shocked when they recognized who he was.

"Treasonist!" one of them shouted.

At that, the Lead Rider, Maya, snapped her head up. Her

helmet hung down over her nose, but Hux could still read her eyes through the slits. She was conflicted. Confused. Torn.

"Shall we arrest him?" one of Maya's Riders asked. But it was more of a beg. He *wanted* to arrest Hux.

Maya hesitated. She locked eyes with Hux.

Hux shook his head.

"Let's not lock him up yet," she finally ordered. "Let's see what he wants."

Hux let out his own breath. Thank Protection. Ferrin had said Maya may be on his side. He prayed that Ferrin was right.

He guided his horse right up to the line of Riders. The rioters shouted louder.

"What's brought this on?" Hux shouted to Maya. His horse skittered sideways, tense and alarmed at the rising tension.

"Not here!" Maya bellowed back. "Follow me."

One of the Riders grabbed Maya's elbow. "Don't take this traitor toward the fortress, Commander."

Maya yanked her elbow from his grasp. "Don't order your own commander. Make way for him to get through. Now."

The Riders split just enough for Hux and his horse to squeeze down the street they were blocking. Rioters didn't dare follow for fear of getting slain by one of the Riders' swords. But as Hux passed through, one of the Riders purposefully knocked him, sending him an uninviting message. Hux ignored it, keeping his eyes trained ahead where Maya and her horse were cantering down the cobblestone road. He followed, the cries of the rioters fading behind him.

The fortress towered ahead, gray and massive, masterfully placed to loom over the entire city. Hux assumed Maya was taking him to it, but she cut right, down a side street filled with shadows.

Hux reined his horse after her. "I need to speak with the King, Maya."

Maya halted in the middle of the street. The buildings on each side were tall, covering the sun. The shadows made the air cool and it smelled of must. Hux knew this place. It was a poor section of Raina. Of course the street was empty, because they were rioting. If Leeland was to start a war with the gods, *these* people would be the last to leave the city to find refuge. They didn't have enough to travel and start a new life. A war with the gods would end them.

Hux dismounted. "Maya. I need King Leeland's ear. Please."

She dismounted, too, and removed her helmet. Sweat and dirt outlined her face where the helmet had sat. "The King is dangerous." Her voice cut him to the core. "He's been driven mad by searching for the quill."

"The quill is no use to him," Hux thundered.

She watched him quizzically. "You know where it is?"

"This isn't about the quill. This is about Thãen. And the power of the quill will only work for Naomi Massoud. She has already used the quill. Maya, please. The plan has already been revealed to us. Now I need to set it in motion. I need you to help me set it in motion."

She clenched her fists at her sides. "I believe you, Huxton, but I can't betray King Leeland. I can't lose my position. I know you so easily threw it away, but I can't do that. I—I don't want to throw it away."

"You've already betrayed him by talking to me," Hux argued. "You lied to him when Ferrin asked you to."

"It's just politics. I haven't done anything wrong."

Hux took a brisk step in her direction. "If you don't act against him, The Dark Hand will win. You won't be Lead Rider for long because there will be no position for you to have. Raina will be gone. *Everywhere* will be gone."

Maya stared up at the fortress in the distance. "Raina has stood through many disasters."

"Not this one," Hux begged her to understand. "The Dark Hand is coming, and when it does, it will have no mercy."

Maya lowered her gaze to Hux again. Her chin dropped and she sighed. "What do you need me to do?"

Hux would have smiled if he weren't so stressed. "Raina's rivers are the key in all this. The red color of our rivers is because of ink. We knew this, sort of, but now we know why. It was Protection's doing. The rivers here connect with underground tunnels that lead to Le'Gar. Somehow the rivers here need to be released into those underground tunnels, because we need to flood out Le'Gar. The ink will blot out Calamity."

Maya blinked, speechless.

"I'm telling the truth," Hux said with a desperate breath. "Le'Gar is evacuating as we speak. Naomi is going to draw Calamity to Le'Gar and trap it there with the help of the gargoyles. We *need* Raina's rivers to be released."

Maya shook her head, and all she could say was, "Ink?"

"Yes, Maya. Ink! Protection is going to write Calamity out of our story. It's blotting it out like an idea that's been written on paper then scratched over. Don't you understand? I know it's hard to grasp, but the ways of the higher beings aren't always clear. We just have to accept that they work in ways we are incapable of comprehending."

"And trust that it will work out?" Maya asked quietly.

Hux nodded. "If we want to live, then yes."

The sound of clashing metal came from the direction of the rioters.

Maya's alert spiked. "They're uprising. There is going to be death. They don't want to provoke the higher-beings."

Hux reached out and grabbed her wrist. "We have to. Help me figure this out."

She grasped his hand in return. "I know how."

His heart sped. "You do?"

"I only just found it," she whispered. "A coincidence...a mistake..."

"No," Hux said. "A divine occurrence."

Maya pressed her lips together, her nostrils flared from emotion. "We have to go back out the way we came. What I found is in the mountains, just outside the city walls. There's some sort of button at the bottom of one of the river-beds. It's more so a creek, a run-off from one of the main rivers. And an underground tunnel...I saw one...when I fell."

"Take me to it," Hux demanded.

"The other Riders are going to see me leading you out of the city walls," she said with dismay. "They may try to follow."

"Let them follow," Hux mumbled. "Let them try to stop me."

CHAPTER FORTY-TWO

Maya charged through the rioters, her horse plowing its way through the thick masses. Hux trailed her, getting rocks to the face and curses slung at him. But he kept his chin down and clung tightly to his reins.

Just as Maya assumed, four of the Riders broke rank and began to follow her and Hux.

Hux swore under his breath and urged his horse faster. He rode side by side with Maya as they tore out of the city into the surrounding mountain. The rioters were behind them now, but in their place were the four Riders at their backs.

Maya was sharp with her reins, leading her horse sideways and cutting around trees in a full canter. Hux did his best to remain as close to her as possible.

One of the Riders shouted. "Commander!" His voice grew angrier. "Commander!"

Maya ignored him.

River grass and ground ferns started to populate the forest floor in bigger clumps. They were nearing the river run-off.

An arrow flew past Hux's ear. He ducked and yelled, "Maya!"

But the arrow had already missed her. Thank Protection.

The small river was right ahead now.

Maya didn't stop until her horse's hooves were skittering at the edge of the water. She threw herself off the horse and Hux tumbled off of his own.

The Riders were not far behind.

"Into the water!" Maya ordered, waving a frantic hand.

Hux leapt into the water, nearly losing his balance. Maya helped steady him then collapsed to her knees, the water rising to her stomach.

"It's down here somewhere," she said in panicked breaths. "Feel for it. It's under leaves. Find it!"

Hux dropped down, the water splashing him in the face. He used his good arm to feel around desperately. His fingers touched slimy leaves and pluff mud, but nothing button-like or solid.

The Riders reached the river. All four of them dismounted and bolted to the water's edge. Two of them held cocked bows and arrows, aiming them at Hux and Maya.

Maya stood between them and Hux, chest flaring.

"Don't be unwise, Commander," one of them taunted. "King Leeland didn't order you to be friendly to our treasonist, did he?"

Maya shook her head, swallowing.

Hux kept digging around the river bottom.

"Then you've committed treason as well," the Rider growled, aghast.

"King Leeland has lost himself," Maya whispered. "We've known this for a while now, and we've let it go on for too long."

The Rider's voice rose. "This isn't about Leeland! It's about *Raina*. We stay true to our land. Through wrong and right."

"No," Maya said, a tear touching her bottom eyelash. "It's never okay to do wrong."

Hux shook, fearing he may never find the button at the bottom of the river. Maybe Maya was mistaken. Maybe she didn't see anything at all and he had just run himself to his own capture.

"I'm sorry, Commander," the Rider said softly. "You were a good leader, but I stand with Raina."

He released his arrow.

It struck her through the core.

"Maya," Hux whimpered as she toppled into the water.

He reached for her, holding her head above the surface.

"Let me go," she gasped. "Keep digging."

"No," he whispered.

"Do what I could not," she begged.

Her eyes fluttered closed and her breathing grew shallow. Then she went still.

Another arrow flew, striking Hux in the arm.

He cried out and dropped Maya. Then he drove his hand back into the water, shakily scanning the bottom.

Please! He begged. *Please!*

Another Rider jumped into the river and drew his sword.

Hux's hand bumped something solid. The button.

The Rider lifted his sword.

Hux pounded his fist into the solid circle. It pressed in.

The ground shook. The river-bank rattled and loose dirt tumbled down into the water.

The Rider drove his sword through Hux's chest.

A geyser-like eruption of water shot into the air. Then another and another, like holes being poked in the river. Then the water started to drain, seeping through the holes into a place underground. Into the tunnels that led to Le'Gar.

Hux sat in shock, the sword stuck in him below his sternum. The world was blurry.

Above him, the Rider smiled down at him. "Not wearing a

chest plate, treasonist? What a shame. A poor decision if I ever knew one."

Then Hux toppled over beneath the water.

He closed his eyes and was keenly aware of how cool the water was against his face. It was silent under the surface. Peaceful. He thought of Vira and Millicent. They were his future no more. He thought of Naomi. He prayed for her.

Then he inhaled a deep breath of water and let it drown his lungs.

Soon the light was gone from his eyes.

But the river was lowering.

He had succeeded.

CHAPTER FORTY-THREE

"Naomi," Ferrin whispered.

Naomi awoke with a start. Ferrin's hand was on her shoulder. She ached with fatigue and hunger clawed at her stomach. The street she had fallen asleep in was empty. Abandoned. Completely evacuated.

It had been two days since Hux left for Raina. The storm had raged the entire time, only slowing for an hour or two at a time. The rain was soft and the wind calmer. Right now was one of those slow moments.

Naomi had fallen asleep, leaning against a stone wall under the protection of the wing of the gigantic griffin that used to perch above the cathedral. Le'Gar crawled with gargoyles now. They slunk through the streets, pacing, waiting for the moment when they would have to act as a barrier to trap Calamity. The ones with wings soared frequently, enjoying the freedom of the sky that they hadn't had since their arrival in Le'Gar. But this griffin had taken to staying by Naomi's side. On the ground, he was larger than she thought he was. He towered over her by nearly five feet, and his wingspan was probably twelve. He still didn't speak, but his body language told her that he was there to protect her and the others. A silent stone shield.

The evacuation had been successful. Le'Gar was a ghost town. Vira had taken up the responsibility of leading the thousands into the mountain. She had claimed she didn't know exactly where they would take refuge, but they would be safer on higher ground, even if that meant no shelter. No matter what, Naomi knew they would be in safe hands with Vira. And when Hux returned from Raina, they would have another protector. Naomi was sure of it.

But here in Le'Gar, it was just her, Ferrin, Deirdre, Eli, and the gargoyles. Ferrin had started a fire in a barrel under the safety of the griffin's other wing right before Naomi fell asleep. The sun had been up, but now the world was darkening.

"Is it time?" Naomi asked.

Ferrin crouched in front of her and nodded. "The waters are coming."

Naomi bolted upright. "How do you know?"

Eli appeared over Ferrin's shoulder and Ferrin rose to be even with him.

With both of them staring down at her, Naomi felt an anxious tug in her core. "What?" she asked. "What's happened?"

Ferrin tipped his head toward Eli, not able to say it himself.

Eli's gray beard twitched. "Hux was successful in releasing the rivers. I saw him in a vision."

"Okay, great," Naomi applauded, standing now. "How long do we have until the waters get here?"

"Not long," Eli admitted. "We have to act quickly. We have to get this right. We can't let Hux's death be in vain."

Naomi froze. Her throat closed. "What?"

Ferrin clenched his jaw and nodded with watery eyes. "It's

true, Omi. He's gone. I saw it myself. Both Eli and I did." He hung his head. "A shared vision is always true in some way."

"No, it—it wasn't supposed to happen that way!" Naomi choked. "All he had to do was—was—"

"All he had to do was start the war," Ferrin said softly. "There was always a risk. He knew that."

Naomi covered her face with her hands. "*No*. He was family. He—he can't be gone."

Ferrin wrapped his arms around her and held her close. "I'm sorry. For him, for you, for Vira..."

Naomi looked up at Ferrin, eyes still soaked. "Vira. She's going to be heartbroken."

Ferrin sighed. "She will be. But war doesn't care about broken hearts. No matter what's happened to Hux, the waters are coming and you still need to get Calamity here. We have to keep going."

Naomi stepped away from him and looked up to the sky. The clouds were a pale gray, the rain faint.

"I need the storm to be stronger," she said. "If I'm going to drag a supreme being from the void into our world and keep it trapped, I need a monstrous storm. One that could rip Le'Gar apart."

Ferrin nodded, understanding. "Let's get you to the cliffs."

Naomi reached back and helped Deirdre to her feet. The librarian moved slowly, like every turn of her head and bend of her knees hurt.

"Will you be able to keep up?" Naomi asked softly.

Ever since Deirdre had revealed the plan, her mortality was fading. She was becoming more and more like stone. Heavy and stiffer.

"I'll keep up for as long as I can," Deirdre replied honestly. "I may not make it to the cliffs."

The storm picked up. A low rumble of thunder roared in the distance. A gust of wind swept through the abandoned street.

Ferrin offered his arm to Deirdre. "Let's go. The storm is ramping back up. Let's get Naomi where she needs to go."

The four of them broke into a brisk trot, the griffin clunking behind them. With the city empty, they were able to make their way easily. The debris from the world's tips offered obstacles, but even when they came to a section of road that was blocked off by a fallen pillar, Eli and Ferrin were able to push it out of the way with their energy forces.

All along the way, gargoyles in the streets watched them. They twitched in anticipation, their gnarly shoulder blades hunched, ready to pounce. Ready to act.

"Soon," Naomi whispered to them as she swept by. "Be ready."

They were in the center of the city when the wind picked up. It was a gust that nearly swept Naomi off her feet. She instinctively grabbed onto Eli's elbow when it ripped through the street. A monstrous boom of thunder shook the ground. A crack of lightning seemed to split the sky in two.

Naomi steadied herself against Eli. "How much farther to the cliffs?"

Ferrin looked up to the pine trees in the distance. "We're only halfway."

Rain began to fall in large splotches.

Naomi felt the energy of the storm surge through her body. It enticed her. She flexed her fingers, reaching for little grasps of it. It willingly obeyed her call. This storm was created for her. Whether it be by Protection or by circumstance, she knew it was for her.

"Can I start now?" she asked Ferrin, pleading with her eyes. "I can do it. I know I can."

"I know you can," he agreed, "but if you start now, you

won't be protected from the flood. If you can control the storm from the cliffs, Le'Gar can be drowned without you in it."

Naomi nodded and continued to trudge on. Ferrin was right. If she wanted to see Thãen in its era of light, she couldn't be in Le'Gar when the flood arrived. She had to see this to the end.

But another explosion of thunder took over the sky, this time sending tremors through the entire city like an earthquake.

The griffin let out a gritty screech as the roof of a tall, skinny building cracked and came crashing down in bits as big as boulders. Naomi didn't have time to move, but the griffin threw its stone wing over her as the boulders slammed against it.

Ferrin yanked Deirdre out of the way, falling backward with her in his arms.

Eli wobbled, the quakes of the city unsettling him.

"Naomi!" Ferrin shouted over the sound of the boulders cracking against the ground.

Naomi had her hands over her head, ducking, but nothing touched her. The griffin's wing hovered over her, and the loyal gargoyle remained that way until all the bits and pieces of the roof were done falling.

"I'm fine." Naomi patted the griffin's leg, then stepped back out from under its wing.

Eli pulled Deirdre up, and Ferrin pushed himself to a stand. The rain fell around them in faster beats now.

There was a groan from somewhere deep within the city walls. It shivered the ground. The vibrations crawled up Naomi's legs.

"What's happening?" she whispered.

Eli's eyes were wide. "The waters," he said in a hush.

Behind Naomi, a crack sliced through the ground, nearly two feet wide. Up from the crack came a rush of red water. It spilled into the street in a constant flow, rushing over Naomi's feet.

Another crack split the street a few feet ahead of them. More water rushed up.

"We aren't going to make it to the cliffs," Ferrin said in a panic.

The whole city continued to tremble. The thunder intensified. Wind howled.

"I have to try," Naomi called through the screams of the storm. "You guys get out."

The gargoyles started making strange gritty noises, as if communicating with each other. Slowly they began to filter to the outer parts of the city. The griffin, who was right by Naomi's side, nudged her shoulder then leapt up to the sky.

When Naomi stared upward, she saw a dome of gargoyles hovering over the city. The sky was visible, but only in wide cracks between each gargoyle wing.

"I'm not leaving," Ferrin bellowed. "I'm going with you."

Naomi had no reason to argue. If she outran him to the cliffs, so be it. If he wanted to follow, that was on him. But either way, if she wanted to get out of the city before it flooded, she needed to run *now*.

To their right, the side of a building split and a spout of water rocketed out.

Eli lifted a palm and held the water back. It pressed against his invisible energy, but he kept it tamed.

"I'll hold off what I can," he promised, though he was straining. "How long do you think you need?"

"I'm fast," Naomi stated. "Can you give me ten minutes?"

The sweat on Eli's forehead spoke for itself, but he nodded. "Go."

So she did what she knew how to do best. She ran. Just like her mother taught her.

Ferrin ran shoulder to shoulder with her. Deirdre did her best to stay close. Even though she was losing energy, she put all of her effort into trailing Naomi.

The ground continued to quake. Cracks split the streets. Buildings threatened to topple. The water underneath the city soon wouldn't hold. Naomi could feel it. Energy pulsed and roared beneath her feet. The waters wanted to erupt. With every passing second, the waters grew stronger than the stone holding it back.

A thunderous crack rang out as a pillar ripped away from the legal building. It began to fall, in slow motion, its heavy mass coming down right over Ferrin and Naomi.

Naomi shoved Ferrin out of the way. He landed on his side, just out of reach from the pillar, but Naomi didn't have time to escape. She ducked and covered her head instinctively, but she knew her bones would crush beneath the weight of the stone. She prepared for an impact that never came. Right before the pillar reached her, it collided with something else right above her. Something solid. Something also stone.

The pillar broke in two, splitting above her head. Naomi peered up in shock as a fully stone Deirdre towered over her, taking the impact of the pillar. Deirdre's angel form cracked in half as the last bits of pillar ricocheted off of her.

Naomi grabbed Deirdre, trying to hold her together, but it was useless. Deirdre was breaking off in bits, falling to the street as rubble.

More of the legal building began to chip away and rain toward the ground. Pieces of stone pelted Naomi.

Ferrin crawled his way over to her and stood, pulling her away from the crumbling Deirdre. "She's gone," he rasped through the dust caused by the falling building. "Naomi, we have to keep moving."

Reluctantly, Naomi removed her hands from Deirdre and

watched as the stone angel collapsed to a pile. She let Ferrin pull her away, because water in the street had risen to her ankles and continued to rise at a sickening pace. And when another roar of thunder took over the entire sky, Naomi knew the storm was strong enough for her to pull in Calamity.

"We aren't going to make it to the cliffs," Naomi said, accepting defeat. She held onto Ferrin's hands. "I'll have to do it from here."

Ferrin gripped her hands tight. He was shaking and soaking from the rain. Water dripped off his nose and into his eyes, but he kept his stare fixated on her. "I'll be at your side."

Naomi grabbed the front of his drenched shirt and pulled his mouth to hers. She kissed his rain-stained lips and whispered, "I love you."

He clung to the back of her shirt, gripping her like she was about to slip away. "I'm desperate to live," he choked. "If only to share a life with you."

Naomi parted from him and firmly held his face in her hands. "Then let's live."

With Ferrin at her side, she closed her eyes and turned her palms upward. The storm was a monster around them. Wind threatened to tear down the highest steeples of the city. Rain fell in sheets. The thunder itself shook the world like Thãen was nothing but a bag of rocks. In the sky, the winged gargoyles screamed and bellowed. They dipped in and out of each other, waiting for Calamity to be ripped from the sky. To be pulled in from the Void.

As Naomi inhaled, she felt the power of the storm fill her body. It was so intrusive and so overwhelming that for a moment she forgot to breathe again. She grew lightheaded and tipped sideways, but Ferrin was there to hold her up. He nudged his shoulder into her, keeping her steady.

Naomi snapped her eyes open and tipped her head to the

sky. *Rip it open*, she ordered the wind. The wind shook the city as it began to compact, colliding into one big force of energy. It spun and chugged upward to the storm clouds where it pierced a hole right through the sky. Like a pin-prick through cloth. A burst of black shot through the hole in the sky, glittering like light. The sight of it almost paralyzed Naomi. No one had ever seen the Outer Void before. But she couldn't dwell on its beauty when she was holding the power of the sky in her hands. Her whole body tensed and she dug even deeper within herself. *Rip. It. Open.*

The black hole grew. It widened like a screaming, open mouth. The gargoyles in the air parted, making way for the entrance to the Outer Void. Naomi used the wind's energy and started pulling from the Void. She tugged with her mind, knowing Calamity was in there somewhere. *You can't hide from me,* she viciously thought.

Lightning flashed and illuminated the black hole. That's when Naomi saw the silhouette of a black hand writing within the Void.

She began to pull harder. The fatigue of wielding nature made her legs weak and she fell to her knees. But her knees were only on the flooded ground for one second because Ferrin grabbed the back of her shirt and hauled her up. She tried to regain her balance but all of her energy was being thrusted into the Void, and her body wanted to give up. Once again, she dropped, but Ferrin held her up by the waist.

"Come on, Naomi," he said right into her ear. "You're doing it. You're almost there."

With Ferrin holding her up, she threw every ounce of energy she had at the Void. And the sky darkened as, at last, a five-fingered hand emerged from the Void.

CHAPTER FORTY-FOUR

The Dark Hand stretched from the mountains, across the entire city, and out into the sea. It was larger than Naomi had ever imagined it to be. The black of its shadow was thick as smoke. It curled its fingers, like it wanted to reach down and swipe Le'Gar off the map, but Naomi used the energy from the storm to force its fingers back open.

The airborne gargoyles began to collectively create a barrier around the Dark Hand. As they worked, Naomi pulled Calamity down closer to the city. It tugged against her, trying to get back to the Void, but she pulled harder. She had it down to the rooftops when water splashed against her shins. All this time she hadn't realized the waters were rising in the city.

She looked down and saw that the entire street was shallowly filled with red water. With panic in her eyes, she looked to Ferrin.

He didn't have to say anything. She knew he could read the realization in her eyes: They weren't going to make it out of the flooded city.

"Ferrin—"

"Just keep going," he demanded. "We'll leave this world together."

Naomi pulled and pulled. Calamity fought against her. Sometimes Calamity won, ascending a few feet before Naomi dragged it back down again. But every time she got Calamity closer and closer to the city, the gargoyles took advantage and inched upward to surround the Dark Hand. Ever so slowly they were creating a barrier between Calamity and the Void.

Calamity was almost within the city walls when a roar erupted from the side of the city that faced the mountains. For a brief moment Naomi looked in the direction of the sound, and she saw, rushing down the streets, a massive flood of red. Like a dam had been let loose at the city gates. And the flood was heading right for her and Ferrin.

Naomi dug her heels into the ground and pulled with all the strength she had left. Calamity writhed under her force. It seemed to know it was going to lose. With one last effort, Naomi forced Calamity into the city. Its form covered the entirety of the city, filling it with black shadows and the chill of death. And when Naomi couldn't hold onto the Dark Hand any longer, she let go.

Finally free of her grasp, Calamity levitated upward, but it was met by a wall of gargoyles who covered the sky. The gargoyles pushed the hand down again, forcing it to remain in the city.

The flood of water ripping through the city tumbled nearer now. It roared like a mad sea, but Naomi wouldn't stop it with her powers. The flood had to blot out Calamity. If she saved herself, she would be forsaking the world. So she and Ferrin ran in the opposite direction of the waters.

They charged toward the cliffs, aiming for higher ground. But it was obvious that they couldn't outrun the flood. Behind them, the deep bellow of the Dark Hand shook the city as the flood overtook it. The water around Naomi's legs were getting higher and the drum of the oncoming flood behind her was louder now.

Half the city was already gone. Soon she and Ferrin would be, too.

Naomi kept running, keeping her eyes fixated on the cliffs in the distance. She would run until the flood caught up to her. She would leave this world running.

The sound of the flood was upon them now.

Naomi took a deep breath and accepted the worst.

But Ferrin tore away from her side. He let Naomi get a few paces ahead of him, then he stopped in the middle of the street, faced her, stood tall, and let the flood hit him.

Naomi turned just in time to see the wall of water slam him, but it didn't consume him. Instead, the water acted as if it had hit a massive wall. It stopped against Ferrin, shooting upward to the sky. Ferrin stood still and firm, his body small against the monstrous wall of water he was holding back.

For a moment Naomi couldn't move. She simply watched as Ferrin single-handedly held an ocean back. For her. For them.

Then she took control of the water with her mind and sent it tumbling back the way it came. Back toward Calamity.

As the water receded in angry waves, Ferrin sprinted toward her and together they ran for the cliffs.

As they ran, the sky broke open where Naomi had ripped it through to the Outer Void and a golden light exploded out of the rip. The light covered the sky, the city, the mountain, the sea. Le'Gar was drowned, and with it went Calamity.

By the time Ferrin and Naomi reached cliffs and began to climb into the pines, the rooftops of the city had disappeared. The flying gargoyles had retreated to the Outer Void and any grounded gargoyles had accepted their fate to the flood.

But Ferrin and Naomi had made it to the cliffs. And when

they stood at the lookout, nothing but dark red water was below. Even the King's cathedral was gone, underwater.

But so was Calamity.

Shaking with fatigue, Naomi collapsed into Ferrin's arms. He held her against himself and dropped to his knees, too exhausted to keep both of them upright. Naomi was soaking wet, her muscles trembled and cramped, she couldn't get a proper breath, but her body was against Ferrin's and his heartbeat thumped against her ear. It was the safest she ever felt and if she could stay like this forever she would.

Ferrin held her tight, trying to catch his own breath, but he managed to find enough strength to lift her face so he could see her. "We did it. Calamity is gone."

Naomi could do nothing but hold back tears.

"Thãen is safe now because of you," Ferrin said.

"We all destroyed Calamity, not just me."

"But none of us could have done it without you. I'm so proud of you." He gazed at her with longing. "I never imagined I would fall in love with a god."

Naomi smiled, but it faltered. "How much longer do you have here?"

Ferrin rested his chin on her head. "I don't know, Naomi. But I'm here right now. Let me love you while I'm still here. Don't think about tomorrow. Today has had enough troubles of its own."

CHAPTER FORTY-FIVE

Naomi and Ferrin headed into the mountains, but they looked back a few times to see what was left of Le'Gar. From their elevated view, they couldn't make out a distinction between where the sea ended and where Le'Gar started. It was all covered. Le'Gar belonged to the Desarian Sea now.

They found tracks in the mountains, telling them which direction the people of Le'Gar had fled. They followed the trail.

"Where do you think everyone will go?" Naomi asked quietly.

"They'll have to scatter," Ferrin said. "Or start a new territory somewhere."

Naomi stole a glance at him. "Do you think Eli made it out of Le'Gar?"

"I don't know," Ferrin answered sadly.

They hiked in silence, for the first time having no real task ahead of them, no danger at their heels. To Naomi, their wandering felt aimless. She felt somewhat lost again. They had saved Thãen, but now what? What was the next thing? What does a god do? Is a god worthless if they aren't saving?

Ferrin grabbed her hand. "You're worth more than anything to me."

"Are you reading my mind?" Naomi asked in surprise.

"No, but I can feel fragments of your thoughts," he said with a soft laugh. "It's easy to do when I know someone fully."

Naomi's heart swelled. "I hope you get to know me more."

"I hope so, too."

"I'm so afraid you're going to wither away," she admitted in a hush.

"Where do you want to live?" he asked.

Naomi smiled, knowing what he was doing. He wanted her to pretend that he could be here forever. And in his defense, maybe he could. He hadn't gone yet. Could they age together?

"I like the sea," she said gently. "Hux and I spent time right on the coast while we waited for you and Vira."

Ferrin nodded. "Would it make you feel close to Hux if we lived there?"

Naomi held back tears. "Yes."

"Then let's live there." He smiled at her and squeezed her hand tighter. "We can keep his memory alive."

When late afternoon began to turn to evening, Ferrin held an arm out and stopped Naomi.

Her heart sped up. "What is it?"

Ferrin gazed ahead into the trees that were growing darker with every minute. "I feel someone I know."

He lowered his arm from Naomi and strode ahead of her. He began to run when the fading sunlight cast a soft glow on a person sitting on a wide rock.

Naomi ran after him, her heart swelling with joy. Sitting on the rock was Eli. He had made it out of Le'Gar.

Ferrin slowed when he got to Eli. Naomi watched Ferrin's face fall.

"Your hair is whiter," Ferrin said.

Eli looked up with a smile. "Of course it is, I'm old."

Ferrin didn't smile. "You're aging quickly."

Naomi took Eli's hand in hers. "Was it hard to escape the flood? Are you hurt?"

"No." He squeezed her hand. "But I'm finished."

"What do you mean?" Naomi asked with angst.

"Don't say that," Ferrin begged.

Eli shook his head. "It's alright, Ferrin. I'm the oldest Magnificent to ever live. I think I'm ready to be done." He studied Ferrin. "Do you feel well yourself?"

Ferrin looked down at his hands. "I feel...fine."

Naomi bent down in front of Eli. "Do you feel able to travel? Ferrin and I are hoping to find Vira and Millicent."

Eli locked eyes with Naomi. "Do you know, Ms. Massoud, that Thãen will never tip again? It won't so much as rock." He made a tight fist. "It will stand firm in the palm of The Hand of Protection. In Mavelic's hand. The only darkness Thãen will know from now on is the night sky. Even the shadows are harmless now. Because of *you*."

"Because of all of us." Naomi hugged Eli around the neck. "Thank you for your years of protection over my life." She squeezed her eyes shut so she wouldn't cry. "From the moment I stepped foot in Le'Gar, you were there to keep me safe."

Eli's weak arms hugged her back. "It was my pleasure to be your protector." He pulled away. "But now I think you have someone else who will take over the job."

Ferrin reached for Eli's arm. "Come on, let's get you up."

Together Naomi and Ferrin hoisted Eli to his feet.

Naomi held onto Eli's arm with a gentle touch. His bones felt fragile. The first few steps the three of them took together were clunky, and Naomi knew in her heart that Eli truly was nearing the end. She looked across to Ferrin who held onto Eli's other arm. Ferrin met her gaze with sorrowful eyes, but he gave her a small, forced smile.

The three slowly made their way farther into the mountain. Night fell and Ferrin took the lead, guiding them somewhere he knew of well. When they arrived, Naomi let go of Eli's arm and stared in disbelief. Not because the place Ferrin had led them to was enchanting, but because it drew Naomi back to the very beginning of her journey with Ferrin.

Ferrin had led them to the cave in the mountains where he once lived. The same cave he brought Naomi to when he first found her and decided to bring her to Zul. Standing in front of the cave once again was like traveling back in time. Being here was hurtful and joyous all at once. Joyous because the darkness that clung to Thãen when Naomi was first here was gone now. Hurtful because the first time Naomi entered this cave, she hadn't met Hux or Vira yet, and now Hux was dead and Vira was somewhere unknown.

"Would you like to rest inside?" Naomi asked Eli.

Eli nodded.

Ferrin and Naomi took Eli into the darkness of the cave. They snaked their way through the narrow tunnel and into the cavernous opening where remnants of Ferrin's things still remained. A metal lantern still had wick and oil and Ferrin lit it. Faint light made shadows dance against the rock walls. The two lowered Eli to the ground, and he smiled as Ferrin shed his cloak and propped it under his head.

"Comfortable?" Ferrin asked.

"Very." Eli folded his hands over his chest. "I think I'll have a rather fulfilling night of sleep."

Naomi sat on her knees at his side. "Do you want us to stay with you?"

"No. Why don't you go back outside and start a fire while I

rest? I feel that Vira may be closer than you think. Light a fire to give her a signal that you're here."

Ferrin lightly squeezed Eli's arm. He sat there for a moment, just staring at the old Magnificent, then he rose and took Naomi's hand. "Let's go light that fire for Vira. She must be looking for us, too."

Naomi clung to Ferrin's hand as they wove their way out of the cave and into the black night again.

"Eli isn't going to wake again, is he?" Naomi whispered.

Ferrin stared blankly up at the luminous stars. The stars shone brighter now that Calamity had gone. Even the night wind didn't feel as ominous. "Probably not."

Naomi hung her head, but grief didn't overtake her. She understood that Eli had been living long enough. He was probably looking forward to eternal rest. She lifted her head and watched Ferrin as he prepared a fire. Would Ferrin's life be over, too? Would he fall into a slumber tonight that is so heavy that he wouldn't wake either?

Ferrin bent and waved a hand over the logs he had set and an orange flame bloomed to life. Satisfied with his work, he sat and turned to Naomi.

She narrowed her eyes. "You said you couldn't create flames."

His smile was soft. "Maybe there is still some awakening in me, too."

When he looked at her, she saw all the versions of him that she knew. The stern, closed-off rescuer who found her outside of Le'Gar, then her unlikely partner who somehow turned into her friend, and now the person she loved. And the way he was looking at her made her think he saw the same things, too. Like their time together was flashing before their eyes. Just like it does before you die.

Naomi ran to him and dropped to her knees. She hugged

him and he pulled her onto his lap. She clung to the back of his shirt, the fabric embedding beneath her fingernails. He kissed her forehead, her jaw, her neck.

His lips on her skin made her shiver, but she was anything but cold. Her cheeks were hot and her insides burned. Her hands found their way to the front of his shirt and she unbuttoned it, holding her palms against his chest. His chest rose and fell in anxious breaths. Naomi loved the feel of it. It meant he was alive. It meant he was still hers.

Ferrin held her hair back and kissed her lips. Naomi pressed in, her body fully flushed against his.

"Wait," Ferrin whispered.

Naomi slowly pulled away to look at him.

He brushed a thumb over her cheek. "After a lifetime of regrets, I want to do this right."

"Okay." She touched his chest again, just to make sure this was real.

"Will you marry me?"

Naomi rested her forehead against his. "Of course, ranger."

"Don't call me ranger, Ms. Massoud." He smiled.

"You're supposed to call me Ms. Smyth. It's part of the fun."

He shook his head. "I can't do that. I can't mock a god."

Naomi stared at his lips. "I don't care what you do. As long as you're mine."

"I'm yours."

"For how long?" she asked fearfully.

"For as long as we get." He kissed her again, holding her face gently in his hands.

"I pray that Protection sees fit for you to stay." Her breath hitched. "I beg of it."

"Me, too."

They lay together by the fire, waiting for Vira to arrive, or waiting for Ferrin to drift away. But as the night went on, Vira never came, and Ferrin stayed. When the waiting became too cumbersome, Ferrin's eyes closed and he dozed off. Naomi lay right beside him, watching his breathing. Sometimes she rested her fingers on the pulse in his neck to reassure herself. She stayed awake as he slept, willing him to stay. She was a god. Perhaps she had a say in what happened to him. Perhaps her prayers were powerful.

At one point in the dead of night, a rush of cold wind blew out of the cave. It startled Naomi and she sat up as the surrounding trees stirred. A faint, translucent, blue light drifted out of the cave's mouth and dissipated into the air.

A soft whisper echoed around Naomi's ears. *Goodbye.*

Naomi knew Eli was gone.

But Ferrin kept breathing.

Finally, when Naomi couldn't keep her eyes open anymore, she placed herself in Ferrin's arms and held him with her cheek against his chest. The slow rise and fall of his breathing lulled her to sleep. At least if he died tonight, he would die in her arms.

CHAPTER FORTY-SIX

Ferrin opened his eyes. He hadn't realized he had drifted to sleep. The wooden chair beneath him wasn't even that comfortable, but the sound of the sea coming through the open window in front of him and the sleeping baby on his chest had been enough to send him into an afternoon snooze.

A warm summer breeze blew into the seaside home, and Ferrin laid a hand on the fuzzy, black-haired head of his newborn son to keep the breeze from waking him. The babe's eyes stayed closed, his lips parted slightly as small puffs of air touched Ferrin's bare chest with every little breath.

Ferrin watched his son sleep, his heart swelling with pride and thankfulness. His eyes drifted to the shore just outside the window, searching for Naomi. She had gone out for a walk. Caring for a newborn, Ferrin had learned, was a difficult task. Especially for Naomi. Apparently motherhood is even difficult for gods. Ferrin had forced Naomi to leave their little cottage for the afternoon. Though Naomi hardly complained, Ferrin could tell she was exhausted and getting restless. He had told her to take her time on her walk and even encouraged her to use her powers a bit. To make flowers grow. To make the sea dance. But she swatted him and told him yet again that she would do no such thing. Ever since Naomi had defeated Calamity, she hadn't used her powers again. Ferrin didn't understand it at first, but he did now. Naomi wanted nothing more than a normal, modest life. She didn't want to be a god. At least, she didn't want to be a practicing one.

The baby on Ferrin's chest stirred and opened his eyes. He looked up at Ferrin with sleepy, dark blue eyes.

"Hey, Elias," Ferrin whispered.

Naomi had chosen the name. Elias Huxton Massoud. Named after the oldest Magnificent to ever live and the bravest Rider who gave his life for the greater good. And though Naomi would never say so, Ferrin knew giving Elias the surname Massoud meant he was also named after the strongest woman to ever walk Thãen's grounds.

As Ferrin watched the waves slowly crash against the sand, a voice he hadn't heard in quite some time whispered telepathically into his brain.

Wake up, ranger. Someone is excited to see you.

CHAPTER FORTY-SEVEN

Naomi walked barefoot on the sand. The waves lapped at her feet and she watched the salty water cover her toes. Sometimes, out of curiosity, she'd ask a wave to avoid her at the last minute. The water always listened, receding before it hit her skin. She wouldn't admit it to Ferrin, but using her powers, even in this small way, was exhilarating and refreshing. It reminded her who she was. It reminded her that she was no longer lost.

She stopped walking and faced the sea. Somewhere out there, her first home, Beezus, lay destroyed. She wondered if parts of it had been rebuilt or if Calamity had taken away any possibility of rebuilding. But Zul was rebuilding, even though its land was all reduced to ash. Maybe Beezus stood a chance. If it did, she would probably never know, because her life was no longer in Beezus. It was here in Blaire, with Ferrin and Elias. The thought made her smile.

She looked up at the blue sky filled with small, puffy clouds. The blue was nearly luminescent. So vibrant. It had never been that blue when Calamity existed. Naomi never noticed how shaded the world had been. Even on the brightest days there had been shadows. Not now, though. Now there was golden sunlight and crystal-clear water. Even when it stormed, the gray clouds were silver. Thãen was beautiful again. But even more importantly, safe. And even though nearly two years had passed since the flooding of Le'Gar, Naomi continued to be astounded by the beauty all around her. The beauty of Thãen and the beauty of her new family. Her husband and son.

"Naomi!" a voice in the distance cried in excitement.

Naomi looked up the beach, where two people were silhouetted by the sun's brightness. One of the people was running toward her, the other walking slowly behind.

Beaming, Naomi took off toward them. She couldn't go too fast because she was still recovering from birthing Elias, but she couldn't contain herself. She hadn't seen these two in months, and she couldn't get to them fast enough.

She collided with Millicent, who had sprouted quite a bit in the past year, and the girl threw herself into Naomi's arms.

"Careful, love." Vira caught up, smiling just as big. "Naomi is still healing."

Naomi kissed Millicent on the forehead then stepped back to see her fully. "You've grown!"

Millicent stood tall. "I have. I had to get new shoes." She lifted a foot. "Like 'em?"

"I adore them." Naomi examined the shoe. "They look very expensive, or rather, very intricately created."

Millicent held a finger over her lips and whispered, "They're special."

Naomi frowned. "How so?"

"Brahm made them."

Naomi looked at Vira with wide eyes.

Vira laughed and held her arms out to Naomi.

"What have you been up to over there in Mira Isla?" Naomi

squeezed Vira tight. "Hanging out with dead friends and buying magical shoes?"

Vira let go of Naomi and nodded. "What did you expect of me?"

"Nothing less." Naomi grinned. "I'm so glad you're here. Both of you."

"Where's Ferrin?" Millicent hopped from foot to foot. "I miss him. Where's the baby? Oh, I can't wait to hold the baby!"

"They're back at the house," Naomi said. "Let me show you the way."

Vira stepped into stride with Naomi as Millicent ran ahead of them to splash in the surf.

"Are you feeling well?" Vira asked.

"I'm feeling well, but motherhood is a lot more difficult than I imagined," Naomi admitted. "Sometimes I'm overly happy, sometimes just downright exhausted."

Vira laughed. "That's normal. How is Ferrin adjusting?"

Naomi looked down at her feet. "He's wonderful. He loves Elias, and he's looking after me well." She looked back up at Vira. "How did I get so lucky to have this life?"

Vira linked elbows with her. "You rescued Thãen. I say you deserve it."

"But you helped rescue Thãen, too, and you didn't get your happy ending."

Vira frowned at her. "Are you talking about Hux?"

Naomi nodded and swallowed a lump. His death still haunted her. Still pierced her heart.

"I see him in my dreams, you know," Vira said softly.

"I see him, too, but I know he's not really there."

Vira smiled. "I believe some of my dreams are reality."

"You mean you think Hux really visits you in your dreams?"

"Hux and I were kindred souls. I don't think even death could take him away from me." She stopped talking to watch

Millicent for a moment. "Millicent asks me about him often. I wish I had more to tell her. I wish Hux and I had had more time together, but he did a noble thing in his death. We wouldn't be here if it weren't for him, and I try to tell him so when I see him in my dreams, but sometimes I wake too soon. Sometimes I can only hug him before he disappears again."

Naomi's eyes grew wet. "But you get to feel him again, even if for a moment."

Vira nodded. "I often can't wait to go to sleep."

Naomi studied Vira. "Funny. I'm often afraid of the concept of sleep. I still fear that one night Ferrin will pass."

"He won't," Vira said.

"How do you know?"

Vira pointed up the shore where Ferrin was a small speck in the distance, waiting for them in the tall grass that sat between the sea and their cottage. "Because he has purpose here again. He's a married man and a father. He's not going to leave you, Naomi."

Naomi watched as Millicent spotted Ferrin and took off up the beach toward him. Millicent's legs never slowed. It seemed she couldn't get to Ferrin fast enough, and Naomi understood the feeling.

When Millie reached Ferrin, she clung to his side and he kissed the top of her head, still holding Elias against his chest.

Naomi and Vira caught up to them and Vira held a hand against her chest when she saw Elias. "He's beautiful."

Ferrin held Elias, who was swaddled loosely in a white blanket, out to Vira. "Would you like to hold him?"

Vira gently took Elias into her arms and stared down at him. "Elias Huxton Massoud. You are destined for great things."

Naomi moved to Ferrin's side and leaned into him. He put his arm around her and pulled her closer. Just like she did every day, Naomi listened to Ferrin's heartbeat beneath her ear. She felt that she always needed the reminder that he was alive. But maybe Vira was right. Maybe Naomi didn't have to fear anymore. Could it really be true that Protection had granted Ferrin the right to live a normal life?

"It's true," Ferrin whispered to her.

Naomi looked up, smirking. "Sneaking into my thoughts again?"

"You're letting me." He rested his chin on her head. "You shouldn't fear so much, Omi. You're a god who can do great things."

Vira tilted her head. "Are you still keeping your powers at bay, Naomi?"

"I am. I don't see the need to make mountains erupt or make seas swell."

Vira nodded slowly and looked down at Elias. "What if Elias inherits your powers? Will you show him how to harness them?"

Naomi smiled at Elias in Vira's arms. "Of course. I won't make Elias go through that discovery alone."

Millie crossed her arms. "What about if Thãen needs you again? Will you help?"

"Will I help?" Naomi looked out at the sea. She could feel its vastness in her chest. Its power surged through her veins. "I'll always help Thãen. If this world ever needs a god again, I'll gladly accept the challenge. I'm a Massoud."

ALSO BY KEIRA F. JACOBS

Daughter of Destiny

Keeper of the Light

Descendant of Shadows

Other

The Testimony of Bendigo Fletcher

ABOUT THE AUTHOR

Keira F. Jacobs grew up in the gorgeous state of Michigan, then planted new roots in sunny South Carolina with her husband. She spends most of her time raising her two boys, exercising, cooking, reading, leading worship at her local church, and writing. Those closest to her know that she loves Harry Potter, the Shire, coffee, gluten free oreos, and almost every genre of music.